PRAISE FOR PHONEME MEDIA'S EDITION OF
SHIKI NAGAOKA: A NOSE FOR FICTION

"*Much like his character's oversized olfactory organ, Bellatin's text exceeds the limits of conventions, deforming language into prose poems, snorting at genre conventions and straining the biographical form almost to breaking point. Yet for all its false pretexts and fakeries, deformations and prostheses, translations and transgression, one breezes through* Shiki Nagaoka *as though it were a thriller...*" **—The Chimurenga Chronic**

"*Games are always a serious matter when they are played by the Mexican writer Mario Bellatin, whose particular brand of sport takes aim at the fine but carefully guarded line between fiction and reality...* Shiki Nagaoka: A Nose for Fiction *is not only a well-constructed metafictional diversion, but also an important new perspective on one of the most creative and controversial writers working today.*" **—Words Without Borders**

"*Impeccably translated from the Spanish by David Shook...*"
—Times Literary Supplement

JACOB
THE MUTANT

by Mario Bellatin

Translated from the Spanish
by Jacob Steinberg

PHONEME
MEDIA
Los Angeles

Phoneme Media
1551 Colorado Blvd., Suite 201
Los Angeles, California 90041

First edition, 2015

Originally published in Spanish as *Jacobo reloaded* by Sexto Piso in 2014

ISBN: 978-1-939419-10-1

Library of Congress Control Number: 2015932627

This book is distributed by Publishers Group West

Printed in the United States of America by McNaughton & Gunn

Designed by Scott Arany

Phoneme Media is a nonprofit publishing and film production house, a
fiscally sponsored project of Pen Center USA, dedicated to disseminating
and promoting literature in translation through books and film.

www.phonememedia.org

Curious books for curious people.

TABLE OF CONTENTS

The Wait

The forms remained in suspense. The men's skin perpetually wet. A golem. A dozen boiled eggs. No mutation was produced. All that appeared was the image of some sheep grazing among rocks.

The Border

Jacob Pliniak is presented to the reader as one of the simplest beings in the world. Considered a rabbi in his small community, he dedicates a good part of his day to teaching Scripture to the village families' children. He is married to Julia and together they own a tavern called The Border. The young Anselm helps them with their tasks. The days are hectic. Jacob Pliniak rises at dawn. Following the ritual prayers, and his baths—fully clothed and with cold water, as if a personal penance—he awaits the arrival of his pupils, who enter the shed out back in silence. Just shortly prior, the bustle in the tavern has come to a close. Many of those present—soldiers and peasants in flight, or women, for the most part, of unknown origin—sleep among the tables, a sleep provoked by the excesses of the night. Julia and the young Anselm have managed the tavern until early morning. They've been attentive to the guests all the while trying their best not to meddle with their conduct. Julia has gone to sleep at daybreak, in the bed that Jacob Pliniak has just left. The wife will not get up until noontime. Before drifting to sleep, making out the sounds of Jacob Pliniak's bath, Julia tends to wonder about that very peculiar way in which her husband does penance. She likewise asks herself why he has never been taken for a legitimate rabbi. In reality, he was not a rabbi in the full sense of the word. If he were, his wife would not be allowed to manage the tavern, even less so until the early morning hours. The Border was perhaps one of the least known works of the Austrian writer Joseph Roth. A complete translation has yet to surface, although fragments have shown up, like the lines offered above, in specialty magazines in Paris and on the West Coast of the States. The Stroemfeld publishing house in Frankfurt holds an old edition in its archives that is believed to be complete, while the independent publishing house Kiepenheuer & Witsch has another version that, many hold, is just composed of a series of fragments. Nobody knows why, but to this day neither of the two has been published. Many exegetes assert that a more thorough investigation has yet to be carried out, one that would allow the compilation of the immense quantity of papers dispersed about that are thought to compose the book in its totality. It is not known what Joseph Roth thought of this novel. Given that he never finished it, he did not live to see it published. One of the women who accompanied him in his final years—an English investigator based out of Paris—

insists that the writer never parted from the text, and that he always went about writing it in a state of complete inebriation. In some way, it seems to be the novel whose editing he reserved for those moments when he was intoxicated. It is a curious fact that, according to the testimony of that very investigator, when he was creating *The Legend of the Holy Drinker* and other texts directly related to alcohol, he would not allow even a pint of beer in his presence while he wrote. That is why this text, *The Border*, may be considered a type of treatise created through the author's unconscious. *There is nobody in the small county of Korsiakov who does not know Jacob Pliniak's tavern*, says one of the book's beginnings. *They all know that, through its only window, it is possible to take in the panorama that spans from the town center, with the towers of that strange, mysterious castle in the background, to the small hut that serves as a border marker. On summer days, as in winter, one can see the hut lit up at night with a faint yellow light—a light that constantly seems to grow closer and then distant—transforming the border into a point of deceptive existence,* the author indicates in another of the text's openings. Both beginnings seem to have been written during Joseph Roth's younger years, when he hadn't yet abandoned his native Galicia. Nevertheless, it would be hasty to consider this text a developmental work, given that, in a certain way, the same narrative lines found in this novel mark his later works as well. There is also the fact that it is a text that the author never stopped writing. For some, Jacob Pliniak's plot takes on an exceedingly basic tone. They think it merely has to do with the story of a shopkeeper, the owner of a border town tavern. The tavern, in reality, is only a cover for an escape route for scores of Jews fleeing the Russian pogroms. Those readers don't seem to pay heed to the adventures that Jacob Pliniak will take part in years later in America, at which point he will even transform into an elderly woman: the pious Rose Plinianson. But getting back to the beginnings, the calm in Jacob Pliniak's life—represented mainly by the religion classes he holds for the children in the region and his weekly incursions to a certain spot on the border to help his religious companions across—is visibly altered (in a definitive way, as will be seen later) when he discovers that Julia, his wife, is the young Anselm's lover. Moreover, the two of them have planned to run away together. When Jacob Pliniak finds out about the incident, guided by the paths left deliberately by his own wife, he feigns ignorance of the relationship. He remains silent, and every morning he faces the breakfast his wife prepares for him before she heads off to sleep alone. A cup of borscht on the table and a teapot placed on the stove is what Jacob Pliniak is accustomed to finding day after day upon waking. On certain occasions he also finds a sandwich made with smoked herring, surely brought from the Baltic the night before by some traveler. Joseph Roth, in his role as creator, goes about pointing out different realities as he proceeds forward with his writing. Perhaps this task is most clearly seen in *The Border*. That could possibly be the reason why it is one of the author's most cryptic and structurally complex works. Maybe that is also why the character, Jacob Pliniak, who in the middle of the narrative transforms into a woman like in Virginia Woolf's *Orlando*, is one of the most curious characters in literary history. There is no doubt that he is, at the very least, the strangest character thought up by our author. Some believe that he is a character who is not entirely complete—that he more so served the author as an inspiration for the construction of other, more complete heroes like the memorable Isaac in *Job*, the shopkeeper Nissen in *The Leviathan*, or the inspector Anschelbum, famous for his zeal in controlling the region's weights and measures. Others think that he is, definitively, an innovation of what was traditionally known as a character. This appreciation can be taken on more clearly by seeing how Jacob Pliniak manages to get the Russian Jews from one side of the border to the other. Thursday is set aside for bringing the exodus to fruition. On those days he does not wait for the students' arrival at his house for study. The people in the surrounding areas know that, apart from the traditional Sabbath, Thursdays have also been set aside as a type of holy day. At dusk Jacob Pliniak makes his way to a point on the border that no one else knows, situated at the ford of a less-than-plentiful river, where he crosses without removing his clothes. The issue of the waters and the clothing forms a part of his personal ritual. According to Jacob Pliniak, each time that somebody bathes with clothes on he is repeating his communion with God. It is not common that someone considered the rabbi of his community be afforded this time for personal interpretations. No less, Jacob Pliniak's behavior is full of actions that, in some way, contradict the Scriptures. He then walks a half an hour to the house of his accomplice, known as the mysterious Macaque, the very one who years later, in New York City, would become the stage actress Norah Kimberley. He returns at midnight, bringing behind him a line of immigrants. Macaque has paid him his share of the money, that those men have given over for his assistance in their escape from the country, in rubles. The following day it will have to be Julia, Jacob Pliniak's wife, who exchanges them in a grains shop where the owners speculate as to fluctuations in the coins of both regions. The immigrants stay hidden for two nights in the tavern. On Saturday morning, the group of refugees is brought up, stealthily, to a wagon driven by a lanky man. In those moments, Jacob Pliniak abandons his prayer room, situated a few yards from the tavern, and goes out to wish the unfortunate luck on their voyage. One of the most surprising discoveries for literature, not just for that of Joseph Roth but for all of twentieth-century literature, seems to be in the mechanism for how a role assigned to a particular character drifts, quite suddenly, into another, completely different one. Precisely when the reader assumes, quite plausibly, not just Jacob Pliniak's presence in the text but, especially, his right to remain in its structure, our character transforms, with no great leap, into his supposed adopted daughter, Rose Plinianson, the highest authority of the women's committee in the town where she lives. It all begins when, without any interruption, at a certain point in the plot, Jacob Pliniak finds himself living in America. He discovers himself in New York City, investigating the whereabouts of the actress Norah Kimberley, well known for her work in the traveling theater groups of the time. Jacob works in a store that markets goods, whose owner is one of the men that he helped cross the border years back. Jacob Pliniak is grateful to God that his ship was the last one able to enter the country without an entry visa required of its passengers. During the voyage, which was on the verge of ending in tragedy when, midway across the ocean, the navigation instruments on the ship broke, he became a spiritual brother to a boy named Abraham. That boy, whose origin lay in the Caucasus region, had witnessed, while hidden among rocks where he usually grazed his sheep, his village being burned down, with its inhabitants enclosed in the small synagogue. The presence in this passage, not only of this spiritual brother, Abraham, but also of the sheep, and above all, the fact that they grazed in a rocky place, stands out. It is apparent that in this part of the story, Joseph Roth is highlighting, in a direct way, the work's mystical nature. Nevertheless, it does not cease to be strange that, during his ship's passage through danger, there is no mention made of any fear of the Leviathan, that deep sea monster present in the majority of tales of this nature. Despite all else, the reference to the rocky place and the sheep is an element that cannot go unnoticed. Two years after his arrival, on one of the busiest streets, Jacob Pliniak stumbles not upon Norah Kimberley, but rather Julia, his old wife. The young Anselm has left her and she has a daughter named Rose. The woman carries out small tasks for community members, but essentially lives off public charity. Jacob takes pity on her. He suggests that they travel to the West Coast together. That is where Abraham Pliniak is living, his spiritual brother, who more than once has sent a letter begging for a reunion. In a very short time, Abraham had managed to amass a small fortune buying land from the few colonists left in the region. He then sold it to a group of refugees seeking a permanent place to settle down and live. Finding his old wife in those conditions seemed to be the sign for Jacob Pliniak to set out on the trip that his brother begged of him. He felt as if he were being given a second chance. He saw in Julia the possibility of having many children—something he had not been able to accomplish in his homeland, mainly due to the constant worry over Russian pogroms. He wanted children capable of passing his spiritual legacy along to future generations. He was even willing to accept Rose as his own daughter. Without thinking twice, he quit his job, picked up Julia and his daughter from the miserable room where they lived, and made the long journey by bus. Abraham Pliniak (nobody knows the reason why, when they became brothers on the ship, he took on Jacob's surname, instead of his family, murdered in the village synagogue) designated a parcel of land to them on the shores of a lake. He then helped them raise a house. Initially, Jacob Pliniak thought of starting up a similar business, a tavern, like the one he had had in Korsiakov. He would rely on his wife Julia, who could help him with administration. They could, by the same token, appeal to a young man with no work, whom they would seek out among the children of the immigrant families, to collaborate. Jacob Pliniak seemed to want, once again, to wake up each day right when his wife, exhausted, sought rest. To find, just as before, his bowl of borscht placed on the stove. Although he would have liked to set up a business that only operated at night, having a tavern again didn't seem like a good idea after all. It would be like returning to the past. He left these plans behind. He was content with the task of spreading the ideas found in the sacred texts. Jacob Pliniak became a teacher once again, very close to what could be considered a rabbi. He once again was close to children. He enjoyed going over, as if for the first time, the most suggestive passages of the Torah and Zohar. This, in turn, reinforced his desire to have children. At this point in the novel, a phrase appears that could be interesting in the context of understanding the author's idea for taking on such a writing exercise. It asserts that, when Jacob Pliniak found out that he would once again interpret the sacred books for the community's children, he said, to himself, that the letters and names are not just conventional means of communication. He asserted, rather, that they are actually the means by which faith carries out its own annihilation. It is precisely at this point, when Jacob Pliniak has uttered such a sentence, that we discover in the text that his work as a rabbi does not endure any great length of time. Nor does his interest in having children, one after another. Many of the families rooted in the region have begun to aban-

don their ancient beliefs. They have begun to try and forget the religion of their ancestors. At this moment Jacob
Pliniak faces perhaps his life's most important crisis of
faith. Unfortunately it is not possible to compare the
passages of this book, *The Border*, with aspects of the pri-
vate life of its writer, Joseph Roth. It will never be known
under what circumstances he conceived any one of the
book's chapters. Bringing forth such an investigation
could have, in some way, clarified certain problematic
aspects of the tale that do not seem at all clear from even
a literary perspective or a mystical point of view. It is only
known that Roth worked on this text constantly, as he
gave shape to other books; and that many of the abrupt
changes in narration were attributable to reasons of a
personal nature... that he even left many of the most sig-
nificant pages lost for good. The fall of the Austro-
Hungarian Empire, the writer's wanderings through
Europe, his adaptation to the prevailing German culture
in Vienna, the rise of National Socialism, his uncontrollable alcoholism and his final condition as a poor and
desperate refugee in Paris—a circumstance that ulti-
mately brings him to a type of suicide—become a kind of
unattainable key to the story. Maybe this is why the
author narrates, at this point, a truly extraordinary event,
that for many holds a relationship to the Jewish Sephirot,
that is, to the sphere of divine emanations, in which the

creative power of God unfolds. It has already been mentioned that Jacob Pliniak has acquired a plot of land on a lake; that he has constructed, with the help of his spiritual brother, a house where he lives with Julia, his wife, and Rose, his wife's daughter whom he loves as if she were his own. It is also known that Jacob Pliniak has become a type of rabbi in a community characterized by its members' slow and steady abandonment of their religion. Despite all of that, at this time he continues developing his personal ideas about water and the body. Thus he continues bathing himself, fully clothed, at unsuspected moments, soaking his feet in trays for hours upon hours, placing his hands in containers of salt water until his skin prunes up. The out of the ordinary fact described by Joseph Roth occurs when Jacob Pliniak submerges in the lake to carry out his daily ritual ablutions. Instants later he returns to the surface, having transformed into his own daughter. But not into the girl that we've known until now, but rather into an elderly woman, eighty years of age. Jacob Pliniak has acquired the body of an old woman, in whose memory the existence of a Jacob Pliniak is perhaps logged, a dead man that drowned while performing his ablutions in a lake upon whose shores he built his house. It's important to point out that in the Kabbalah these transformations that entail person, gender, and time are referred to as "Aphoristic Pools."

The further distanced the person, gender, and time of the transformation, the closer the story comes to another dimension. Perhaps this is why the writer Joseph Roth dares not to just create this very particular episode, but also, just lines ahead, to insist that in the town, the one which the elderly woman Rose Plinianson must now face, hundreds of dance academies have sprung up.

Beatitudes

Joseph Roth indicates that at the time when Rose Plinianson emerged from the waters, the dance schools were a space that took on a greater number of students by the day. In the original text it says that people of the most diverse qualities turned up to that town, with great excitement, in hopes that their lives could occur with a sense of rhythm. They had erected both the typical salons used for rehearsing celebratory parties and a series of grandiose academies where they even taught the steps to tropical music. The competition was so abundant that, with growing frequency, new dances emerged with techniques even more difficult than the last ones. It was oftentimes the norm to resort to such advanced bodily skills that the performances carried with them an air of finding yourself in the rings of a circus instead of a dance studio. After reading these lines, some might find it logical that the publication of a text with these characteristics in the form of a book became impossible. Which is

the motive why Joseph Roth reserved this story for his
moments of inebriation. According to some scholars, the
writing of *The Border* had more to do with a type of prayer
that helped the author not only sanctify the things he
went about indicating, but also to testify as to the secre-
tive world that he had cultivated throughout his life. *The
massive construction of schools was, without a doubt, the
most important business in the region. The main avenue,
aside from the church and the bank, had all other available
spaces dedicated to this activity. The learning methods were
so effective that they became famous in many surrounding
towns. The lines of automobiles that formed on the access
roads were long. It became common to see tourists sleeping
in their cars or even on the street itself. The appearance of
these schools likewise brought about the immigration of a
large quantity of musicians. There were aficionados of prim-
itive instruments and performers of classical music. Someone
even showed up who invented his own instruments, many of
which played themselves. Some of the performers arrived
with their families, who settled down in the camps equipped
for said means. Certain foreigners could not grasp the reasons for which there were no hotels in the region. Few were
those who knew that a decree issued by the women's committee, overseen decidedly by Rose Plinianson, had forbidden
them.* At this point it would be fitting to question the
authenticity of the exact words that Joseph Roth used to

narrate the previous paragraph. At the Kiepenheuer & Witsch publishing house, two versions of this passage exist. Reading the first, which is not the one offered just lines above, one might think that the author treated the story as a finished work... that he wished to prepare the reader for its immediate publication. It is not known where the idea to use dance as the narrative arc capable of transmitting the book's central idea could have emerged from. Perhaps Joseph Roth was seeking—through the curious mixture of mystical and mythical tendencies of interpretation—a theory in which dance played a fundamental role, to express his vision of the collapse of an entire lineage. It is not by chance that the narrative begins in the era of Russian pogroms and ends a century later. Nor that we see how a community of immigrants goes about gradually shedding itself of its ancient beliefs. Joseph Roth does not portray political regimes carrying out racial cleanses—as some authors tend to do when writing on the topic—but rather he presents the facts in such a way that the decision seems to be taken on, and quite naturally, by the inhabitants of a hypothetical town taken over by hundreds of dance academies. The writer affirms in his story that only the houses lived in by members of the women's committee remained free of the influence of the academies. The homes of these characters appear here as if they had been constructed around a lake of stagnant waters. The lake and the houses are shown, in this version, to be an awful-smelling place, plagued by insects, and not the beautiful pool supposedly found by Jacob Pliniak in the first account of the facts, when, following innumerable letters written by his brother, he reaches the area, accompanied by Julia and Rose, his adopted daughter. Even less so as the splendid terrain prepared for him by his spiritual brother, Abraham. The houses, says the author in this part of the story, have been built facing a lake of pestilent waters that host an exaggerated swarm of insects, which would render the development of a normal dance-hall impossible. But living in these conditions does not seem to matter to the members of the women's committee. They have one mission to complete: to close the academies set up in the city. They are not willing to let themselves be defeated and give up their houses, as dozens of families have done in recent years, not only for religious reasons but faced with the offers by the current academy owners. Recently an academy closed down because the committee discovered that the dressing rooms were being used as a place to sleep. They managed to revoke its license, but could not take back the property. The owner was still Pliniak Realty, founded many years back by Jacob's spiritual brother, Abraham, who did not delay in putting it back up for rent. Nor did the committee let a hand touch the community church, which was in the sights of more than one academy. Other spots that the committee managed to save were the boardwalk and the beach. They managed to issue a prohibition against walking in that area with musical instruments or dance costumes. Any strange movement carried out was punished with a fine. To determine when a dance step began to break the law they had set up discrete signs, on which drawings explained the moment in which the movement began to be dangerous. The clarity with which, in this passage, Joseph Roth's unspoken ideas about the apostates of his generation are expressed is astonishing. Since the time he lived in his native Galicia, the writer felt like he was living out the last phases of the Jewish spirit. His past appeared to be getting placed on trial by history, he implies in one of his letters—lost in our times—warning, a bit later on, of the complete obviousness of his interpretation of what had occurred. The deepest evil was not necessarily the one that had put the pogroms into play, he pointed out, but rather the one that would attack the faith of the generations who survived them. Jacob Pliniak also pointed out, immediately after subjecting himself to the day's first ablution, that they needed to proclaim a new way to read the Scriptures. With these affirmations, Jacob Pliniak and Joseph Roth in equal parts seemed to intuit that fate had nothing to do with them. Or at the very least with a religion like the one that they shared. It is not coincidence, then, that just like the penances that Joseph Roth imposed upon himself, mostly character-ized by the long and tortured writing sessions to which he obligated himself—brought forth oftentimes in a state of complete inebriation—Jacob Pliniak soaked his skin whenever the slightest opportunity presented itself. Nor that Joseph Roth would come to affirm that not everything was honesty among the members of the city's women's committee. He writes that, on one occasion, a scandal broke out involving two of its main members: the respectable Rose Plinianson, the transformed daugh-ter, and the reverend Joshua MacDougal, an aspiring priest well known in the region for acquiring the most awing religious conversions purely by means of spiritual songs. It all started to come to light that Rose Plinianson had begun to participate (although, if you take her later testimony to be true, it was almost without intending to) in the academy fever that suffocated the city. To the sur-prise of all, Rose Plinianson created, overnight, her own dance academy. This apparent contradiction, which could appear to be a mistake in Joseph Roth's writing, is possibly part of the reason that the text of *The Border* is not believed to be completed. In the notebooks of the English investigator who accompanied the writer during his final years, certain notes are marked that describe

how Joseph Roth delineated aspects of Miss Rosalyn
Plinianson that specifically pertain to the development
of this passage. It confirms that the woman created her
academy by mistake. What the old woman sought to do
was the opposite, to free the city of the scourge of dance.
She failed to notice that in doing so, she was creating her
own space for dance. The notes assert that Joseph Roth
indicates that Miss Rosalyn Plinianson wanted to carry
out a series of sessions that, feigning dance recitals,
would enable, in reality, the construction of a golem, a
traditional archetypal figure capable of quashing the
invasion they were suffering. That is why she needed
dance; she had even expressed it to the reverend
MacDougal, her spiritual guide. But as the original pages
of Joseph Roth remain lost, little can be done to understand the truth of what went on. It is only known that
Miss Rosalyn Plinianson equipped a small property that
the realtors Pliniak & Co. had abandoned as useless. That
place, hidden behind a rock formation, similar in appearance to the one that saved the brother Abraham Pliniak
from the holocaust that ended his village, had been used,
during the times of slavery, as a maroon colony. As well
as years later as a refuge for clandestine alcohol manu-
facturers. Rose Plinianson cleaned the premises herself
and set up, atop a small table, an old record player that
she had been storing in the basement of her home. Next

to it she placed a modest collection of records of sacred music that she had bought from a traveling salesman that same afternoon when she'd decided to offer her life to her new religion. They went unused, seeing as precisely when she thought to debut them, the women's committee, whose organization was still incipient, issued its first decree, prohibiting its members from listening to music of any kind. Rose Plinianson nailed on the door a notice seeking a painter who usually strolled the city. After that, she disrobed and put on a pair of high heels. She stationed herself next to the entryway, awaiting students. She had already left a handful of crumbs on the table, which soon became a mound of mud, with the intent—she later said in a whisper to the reverend Joshua MacDougal—that the disciples make a doll while they learned the dance steps. It serves our purposes to dwell on this point of the narration for the sake of considering the elements put into play by the author throughout these lines. We would have to take into account, in order to understand the meaning behind what Joseph Roth allegedly seeks to explain, the close relationship between mysticism and magic in the history of religions. It would appear that the figure of Rose Plinianson had been created solely to confuse certain theorists, who would never anticipate finding, in a character with the traits of this elderly woman, a teacher character, that is to say, a master of the Great Name of God, as the divine messengers are known in certain orders. Dance, nude body, sacred music, pedagogy, curse (symbolized by the unstoppable avalanche of dance academies). All these elements linked up, further more, in such a way that they only provide one possible exit: the construction of a golem, a mud automaton that possesses a kind of life of its own, capable of saving not only this captured town but the entirety of a religious tradition. Rose Plinianson's act of switching out the crumbs for mud is, consequently, not arbitrary. The organ music, which begins to emit from the record player, does not seem to be loud enough to call anybody's attention, the author writes almost immediately, as if attempting not to reveal his true intentions. Any sound is drowned out by that produced by the other academies. That may be why the first day is spent alone. Only after a week does it occur to Rose Plinianson to design some informative sheets to point out the exact place where the sessions will take place. At first she tried to make the maps herself. She traced them out in her living room at home. The mosquitos wouldn't let her work in peace. She constantly had to spray the insecticide she kept beside her stove. She took two days to finish them. During this time, the newly founded academy remained closed. At a certain point she gave up. With such imperfect maps, nobody would be able to get around the rock

formation that surrounded the shed where her academy
was located. They were poorly drawn and none of them
looked the same. The following morning she awoke early
and went out to the street dressed in the habit of Sister
Gertrude the Venerated, which she had not worn since
her mother's death. She previously had two holy outfits,
that of Sister Gertrude the Venerated and that of Grace
the Convert. Rose Plinianson had made her mother, Julia
Pliniak, wear the Grace the Convert costume as a shroud.
She dressed her when she was already deceased, despite
her oaths made not to do so during the throes of death.
Rose knew her mother was wrong. Before dying, Joseph
Roth expressed ideas more or less similar to those pro-
fessed by Rose Plinianson. He spoke—before converting
to Catholicism himself—of the necessity of abandoning
old customs. His speaker, the English investigator who
followed him in his final years, transcribed them in the
notebook she always carried with her ("a book of notes
taken" would be a more precise name). Rose Plinianson
was not willing to let her mother burn in the eternal
flames of hell. To rectify that error, following the funeral
she got rid of her adoptive father's kippah and his copy of
the Torah, with which the man had earned a good portion of his living. But unlike the old woman, Joseph Roth
did not have many religious objects with which to part.
Upon going out to the streets dressed this way, some

neighbors looked at Rose Plinianson with awe. The surveyor who lived next door, the old pharmacist, and the seamstress who had her business on the corner all came out to see her walk by. Some made the sign of the cross at her passing, while, at the same time, they turned their backs to her. It might have been necessary to stop at the point of signing the cross and turning their backs, because this far into the story, evil seems to have lost any meaning. Rose Plinianson knew where she was going. She wanted to find the painter who had made the signs on the boardwalk. She knew of potential places where she could find him. More than once she had seen him in the city square drawing the surrounding trees. Or on the beach, ecstatic, facing the waves for hours on end. But where he was most often to be found was on the hill that rose above the central bay. She walked there. Just as she predicted, the painter was there in front of his easel. The palette lay on the ground. The painter therefore had to crouch down every so often to continue the seascape he worked on. That plateau was one of the few places that generations past remembered. From there the old highway could be gazed upon. As well as the beach and the boardwalk. You would have to walk to the edge of the esplanade for the modern buildings to come into view. From that spot two buildings were visible, whose windows shone bright with the sun. All its floors were occupied by dance academies. The rooftops served as enormous dance floors. From the hill the town could be seen in all its splendor. One could never be sure of its true dimensions. From a certain spot it seemed to be a modestly important city, and from another, merely a forgotten ghost town, nothing more. It was situated among farmlands planned out by the area's colonists who, since the earliest times, had considered themselves obligated to decimate the native inhabitants of the region. Abraham Pliniak's deals had been with those colonists, who over time had become a sort of aboriginal people. One member of the women's committee knew that the original settlers, the original inhabitants, had based their social life on the worship of dance. Rose Plinianson interrupted the painter without an introduction. She had little concern for how engrossed he may have been in his work. The artist reacted, leaving a blob on the cloud he was painting. Rose Plinianson asked to go to his house to make the maps. She knew that, in his state, that man could not refuse her offer. It is not known—there is nothing recorded in the English investigator's notebook regarding this detail—whether or not Joseph Roth was conscious of how unusual the meeting was, on that esplanade, between an elderly woman dressed in a religious habit and a man in the midst of a creative trance. Without a word, the painter began to pack his tools. They included a small wooden box. He put away the palette and brushes, after having washed them with a liquid that he poured from a bottle. He then covered the unfinished painting with blotting paper. He then put the canvas and the paper under his arm. Rose Plinianson asked herself how, taking into account his physical features, he could carry so many things. She wanted to help him, at the very least with the easel. The painter agreed and they took it apart together. Rose Plinianson put on comfortable shoes. Maybe they weren't specifically made for the elderly, but they were made with worn leather. The painter began to walk quickly. He walked a few steps ahead of her. They went down to the city together. Rose Plinianson wasn't bothered by the ever-approaching sounds of the academies. She even tried to make sense of them. That practice was similar to the one she attempted when she was silent beneath her wall clock. She always ended up finding some melody. In Korsiakov, before going to sleep, Jacob Pliniak grew accustomed to performing a parallel activity. When his wife Julia left him alone in bed to go tend to the tavern with the young Anselm, he lulled himself to sleep listening to the old clock's tick-tock. In those moments he recreated in his mind the song that every Orthodox mother used, at least until the sixteenth century, to put her children to sleep. A thousand-year-old song accompanied by the rhythm of

the clock was perhaps motive enough to ask a series of
questions: Where could Jacob Pliniak have gotten that
clock from, which lulled him to sleep when his wife left
him alone? And if we start to ask questions of that sort,
why did his wife, during her period of infidelity, insist on
leaving clues so clearly pointing to her relationship with
the young Anselm? Along another line of thought it
would be fitting to ask about the possible link between
Jacob Pliniak's interest in the pogroms and his probable
hindrance from having children. It has to do with questions whose answers will perhaps never be found,
although perhaps the rest of the narration can shed some
light. As is known, the painter walked ahead. Rose
Plinianson followed one pace behind. While she tried to
avoid tripping over the rocks that covered the face of the
plateau, she thought of suggesting to the painter that
aside from the drawings of the map he also create illus-
trations for the lessons she thought to offer. Moments
later she stopped in her tracks. They had already reached
the urban zone. She suddenly placed the easel in the middle of the sidewalk and asked the artist to meet with her
in the shed an hour later. Before taking her leave she
asked him to bring, aside from his tools for painting,
two-dozen white eggs. It was then that she went to visit,
after not having done so in several weeks, her old religion
teacher, Reverend Joshua MacDougal. They had met

years prior, when she was a sort of old little girl and her adoptive father, Jacob Pliniak, had recently disappeared. In those times, they spent long hours seated in front of the church door. As they heard the music from the academies, they seemed to ask themselves how it had been possible for the adopted daughter, Rose Plinianson, to have become the honorable madam, Rose Plinianson, just like that. More than once they questioned, likewise, the true existence of a town like Korsiakov, which Jacob Pliniak spoke so much about up until his final immersion. *Could it be real?* They would ask each other without ever really, of course, agreeing. They spoke on many occasions of the mysterious castle that supposedly stood in that village, of its gloomy towers. Of Rose's mother, Julia, who not only tended to the tavern but also exchanged, in a grains shop, the coins that the trafficker, the mysterious Macaque, gave over to her husband the previous nights. The church was one of the few places where the town's inhabitants could take refuge from the affront of academies. The reverend was not qualified to celebrate mass, but he could rally the parishioners with his songs. He always wore a brown shirt with a priest's collar. Rose Plinianson sat down on one of her favorite benches. The sea breeze entered through one of the windows. The sun fell mostly on the aisle and the walls to the right. A part of the altar remained in shadow. The

reverend had a habit of spinning in the church from
dawn until the final afternoon hours. When he saw Rose
Plinianson, dressed in habit, he could not hold back an
amazed expression. He approached her and kissed one of
the fabric's edges. The sound of the academies became
almost imperceptible in these moments. After a few minutes the reverend went towards the altar. *The eggs that I
have just put on the stove should be ready*, he said as he went
in through a small door beneath the central crucifixion.
Shortly after he came back with a plate of boiled eggs. He
offered one to Rose Plinianson, who declined with a ges-
ture. The reverend lived only on eggs cooked this way. At
this point, again, the story is interrupted. It is the second
time that such an evident break occurs. The first was
when Jacob Pliniak was still running his tavern back in
the border region, and he is suddenly seen working for
some shopkeepers who years back he had helped cross
the border. It is thought that today's missing book passages were present in the original version. They were
turned in to the editor's by the English investigator
immediately following Joseph Roth's death. Nonetheless,
Henriette Wolf, the reader contracted back then by the
Stroemfeld publishing house, purloined several fragments without anyone understanding, until now, the
reasons for such an act. Therefore, the only thing we
have today is the following passage, which describes how

after seeing the reverend offer a boiled egg, the text moves, without any mediation, to reintroducing Rose Plinianson's shed equipped for dancing lessons. It is found lit by some torches soaked in alcohol. The insects, which are allegedly a plague in one version of the tale, have here disappeared entirely. It is not the first time that the reverend is found present in that place. On entering, he recognized the cramped quarters where forty years prior his family's still was set up. In its place, the artist was now seated in front of his easel, contracted to paint the scenes. Likewise we see, on a table, the record player Rose Plinianson had rescued from her house's basement. The room stays quiet. The distant sound of the academies could only be heard as a vague murmur. The artist did not make the slightest movement. A few records piled up on the floor. The reverend drew closer to see what type of music they contained. They were classical symphonies. He hated those compositions. In that instant, from a place not seen, almost as if it had appeared out of nowhere, the voice of Rose Plinianson emerged, requesting that the discs be played. The reverend seemed to avoid using the device. From the darkness, the voice Rose Plinianson insisted. The artist never interrupted his stillness. His outline defined, the shadow his head projected was somewhat elongated. His gaze did not fix on any point. For some time, that man frequented the church quite often. He tended to sit in a spot close to the altar. He had come to the town with a group of workers that were entrusted with the task of converting the houses into academies. Upon seeing him, the foreman flew into a fit of rage. It couldn't be that the contracting company had sent a man like this as a worker—he was missing his left arm. Before dismissing him from the group, he spat on the ground with disdain.

The Wait

The forms remain in suspense. The men's skin perpetually wet. A golem. A dozen boiled eggs. The Stroemfeld publishing house's employee, trying to blot out the traces of the text. No mutation is produced. All that appears is the image of some sheep grazing among rocks.

Explanatory Map, Number 1
by Zsu Szkurka

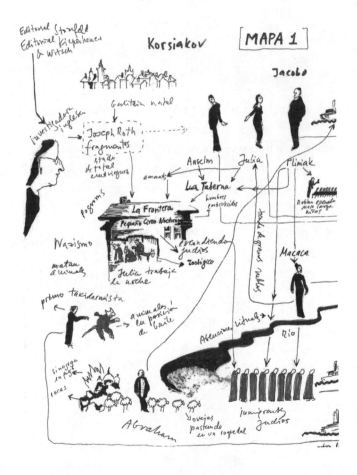

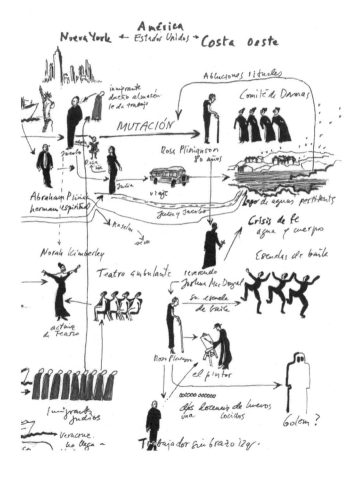

Could There Have Been a Reason for Writing *Jacob the Mutant*?

by Mario Bellatin

A note from the author: any contradictions that may be found in the preceding text may have been consequences of the fact that the text was not originally conceived of in the language in which you now find it presented (nor in the Spanish).

One particular winter morning I remember finding myself standing next to my grandfather.

We were at the zoo.

Before us stood a series of camels.

They were old animals. Sad. Even bored, perhaps.

They had the usual ashen color that their backs show.

My grandfather held my hand tightly.

I never saw him again.

Certainly he died a short time afterwards.

At that time, I didn't really find out if what had happened to him while he was sleeping had been his death—that is what they told me on that occasion and now I have my doubts—or if it had simply been another one of his numerous transformations.

That confusion between death and transformation arose in me some years later, when certain interests of a personal nature brought me to yet again change my religion.

It came back precisely when I was about to convert to a sort of apostate by nature.

I remember that a few members of my family told me in no uncertain terms that my grandfather had suffered a transformation.

Although I am sure that they never clarified what type, I supposed that he had died, as I think it's normal for one to assume given an incident such as this.

I choose to ignore the reasons for which, in that moment, I didn't show a greater interest in what had happened to my grandfather.

That scene—my grandfather standing next to the camels—reappeared in my life many years later.

Fifteen years ago to be exact.

I appreciated that scene in all its splendor as I found myself praying on a particular religious date.

I had already remained in a pure state of prayer for many hours.

I was praying in the precise way that the customs prescribe.

The sheikha of the order I belong to had recommended that I dedicate two full days to repeating the ninety-nine names of God.

To achieve this mission, she presented me with a *tas-bih*—a kind of Muslim rosary—that I was to use just for those two days.

After that time I was to keep the *tasbih* as a sort of relic.

In the exact middle of the trance I submersed myself into with those prayers, the figure of my grandfather standing before the camels in that zoo suddenly appeared.

Not only did I witness the scene unraveling before me in all its splendor, I also felt the emotional weight that the sudden disappearance of my grandfather had brought with it in its moment.

I fell into a deep sadness.

I also remembered—in that moment of spiritual retreat—a story: the story of Macaque, a woman of Slavic origins whom my grandfather often spoke excessively about.

Along with the image of my grandfather and the story of Macaque, also appearing before me was a series of words spoken in another language: Yiddish, the language of my ancestors.

I have never told anyone about that trance into such a particular state of perception.

Nor do I have anyone that I may now ask regarding the relationship that might exist between the figure of my grandfather, the camels, the ninety-nine sacred names of God, and the story of Macaque.

Nor do I have a precise awareness of where this zoo was located.

The only thing that I am certain about regarding its location is that it stood near the sea.

Some could inquire into the relationship that exists between the Yiddish of my ancestors and my current adherence to a mystical order—Sufism—of a marked Muslim spirit.

To more than a few, that alone could be enough of a cause for mystery.

Perhaps that's the reason I now find myself writing these words.

With the goal of clarifying a series of paths for myself, paths of an equally spiritual and social nature, paths that bear great influence on my life.

Just like the writer Joseph Roth—who, as is well known, is the true author of this book—I also experienced, more than once, what is known as a religious conversion.

But unlike Joseph Roth (who simply abandoned his Jewish faith to become a Catholic), I've gone through different transformations.

I've participated in mutations of a spiritual nature, but I don't believe any of them mirrored that of my grandfather, who, as I later came to understand while in a mystical trance in which I found myself completely submerged in water, transformed into another thing (whether animal, plant, or mineral—I'm not certain), so as to continue existing.

Although it has never been clear to me what that new life following his transformation consisted of.

In what pertains to me, my grandfather has never appeared before my eyes in any of his possible variations.

I simply ceased, from one moment to the next, to have him next to me.

I don't want to make room for that widespread scientific idea that matter is not destroyed, but merely changes form. At least not here.

In my family, they continued referring to my grandfather as if he were still right there with them.

For me, he only continued to be present when I recalled the stories he had the habit of telling me during our walks through that zoo.

As I repeated the sacred names in my cell, I came to understand something that had truly previously confused me.

I came to understand that my grandfather was not just that body that had been interred in a grave bearing his name in the city's Jewish cemetery.

I also don't think I fully understood the story of that woman, Macaque, which my grandfather tended to repeat in a way that was almost compulsive.

On some occasions, Macaque was a woman who, like the one who appears in Joseph Roth's texts, was also of Slavic origins.

The existence of this book of Joseph Roth's is peculiar.

Precisely the main theme of that text could be considered conjecture on the art of transformation.

It is possible for it to be read as if it were a tractate on the Sacred Sephirot, with which Jewish tradition, in some way, attempts to quite unsatisfyingly preserve the idea of monotheism and uniqueness.

There is no God but God and nothing exists outside of Him, might be a summary of what it attempts to purport.

Jacob, Joseph Roth's character, was also a rabbi, and one of his missions—which made sense in those times and in those regions—was to educate the children of his village.

What stands out in Joseph Roth's text is that someone who is a rabbi would also obligate his wife to manage a tavern by night, one complete with men in alcohol-induced stupors.

To achieve such a goal—that his wife be willing to carry out a job of that nature—Jacob thought up an attraction: the Tiny Nocturnal Zoo. It was made up of a series of wild animals that he kept in cages and only showed to the public at night.

I chose not to include that element—the Tiny Nocturnal Zoo—in the text known as *Jacob the Mutant*.

The fact that the animals were seen at night doesn't imply that they were necessarily specimens of nocturnal habits, but they served as a pretext for the rabbi to continue operating the tavern.

I ought to clarify that my grandfather never mentioned Joseph Roth or a rabbi named Jacob whose wife worked by night.

Nevertheless, I find it curious that in Joseph Roth's book (which in reality isn't a complete book but rather diverse fragments found over the years in the archives of certain German publishing houses) a character named Macaque also appears, with characteristics similar to those that my grandfather used to mention during our walks near the camels.

Perhaps the coincidence—the name Macaque—was nothing but the manifestation of a collective imagination in the places that my grandfather certainly passed through in his childhood.

According to Joseph Roth, Macaque helped Jacob arrange the escape of groups of Jews fleeing the Russian pogroms that had been unexpectedly brought back in that era.

The tavern also then served as a meeting point, so that the survivors of those pogroms might flee to safer lands.

Macaque helped Jacob ensure that the fugitives continued their flight up until she herself ended up fleeing. Upon reaching New York, Macaque transformed into a famous actress that Joseph Roth named Norah Kimberley.

I am not certain, but I think my grandfather even used, in the same way that Joseph Roth had, both names to refer to that woman—Macaque and Norah Kimberley.

The Macaque that my grandfather always described while standing before those camels was also a woman of Slavic origins. But unlike the woman who helped those fleeing from the pogroms, this Macaque was herself fleeing a horrific marriage, and in a restaurant where she stopped to rest on her way she came across a martial arts expert.

According to my grandfather, this Macaque needed to do nothing more than exchange certain looks, just a few words, to continue the escape from her marital home along with the martial arts fighter.

My grandfather even went so far as to tell me, standing there before those camels, that the fighter ended up being murdered some years later by the police.

The incident with the police occurred after the fighter was accused of making rat-skin shoes.

These things my grandfather tells me can't be true, I remember having thought to myself more than once as a child.

As an adult—in the midst of the mystical process I was going through at the time—I repeated that very phrase again.

But in that moment I also remembered that each time that my grandfather told his stories, I heard—as though they came from almost fathomless distances—something like a chorus of voices articulated in Yiddish.

Do you hear them? my grandfather would say to me, raising his index finger.

All this time I have chosen not to consider the reasons why I was always certain that the words were being said in that language.

Where could they have come from?

How could I have known that they belonged to a language that I didn't even know existed?

After my grandfather would corroborate the existence of these voices (I don't know how he gave such reassurance), he would then explain that Macaque was a woman who referred tirelessly to her lover who had been assassinated so many years prior.

As I already knew from my grandfather's first strolls with me in tow, that man had been a martial arts fighter who, at a certain point in his life, had to flee an international vendetta.

He needed to escape from the Chinese mafia, which at that time had taken over the kung fu filmmaking industry, a genre that reached a certain level of success in the United States.

After the crime, Macaque became a single woman.

According to my grandfather, Macaque's romance with the martial arts fighter lasted about three years.

They settled down in an old boarding house downtown, and the fighter was able to procure a small location nearby to make his shoes.

Perhaps driven by the memory of her marital relationship, Macaque asked the fighter for them not to live entirely together.

My grandfather never explained to me (or at least I don't remember him having done so) why an expert in martial arts would devote himself to the shoe-making industry.

Although it is also true that my grandfather never mentioned who that man was before becoming a martial arts fighter and getting involved in the filmmaking industry.

In reality, I think my grandfather spoke little.

I now have the sensation that he barely murmured just a few scant words.

That's why it seems curious to me that I could have thought that he had told me these stories that I'm now relating during our frequent visits to the zoo.

I am also overlooking the reasons why I thought my family didn't address him as a dead man, but rather as someone who had transformed into someone else.

Getting back to my grandfather and his potential ability, or lack thereof, to express himself, it seems to me that there always remained within me a question as to whether or not he spoke to me. For I felt at every moment that he existed in a different state of reality.

Now that I am thinking about it, my grandfather gave the impression of having become trapped in a kind of eternal present.

In a time when, for example, a string of different languages—both living and dead—were able to converge on a single point: him.

I have always known that my grandfather became bilingual with time.

I was never sure what language my grandfather spoke before reaching our land.

That is to say, his second language—for we know that his first language, Yiddish, was prohibited.

I now feel the need to repeat—as a sort of homage to my grandfather—that Yiddish was strictly prohibited in his childhood environs.

Yiddish could only be used at home.

I am not certain that this scene actually occurred, but one time I saw him performing a kind of dance at that zoo we would visit.

I remember we had gone to take our usual walk on a day with low attendance.

At least I didn't see any other person act as a witness to the dance that my grandfather carried out that day.

As he danced, he repeated, almost like a mantra, that Yiddish couldn't leave their houses.

That it was a language confined to the wooden table where the community's family members ate.

The spectacle of my grandfather leaping and doing something like somersaults on one of the zoo's paths produced a sensation in me that I would describe if I had the talent necessary to do so.

I don't think now is the opportune moment.

I ought to concentrate on the ninety-nine divine names of God.

Curiously, watching my grandfather repeat between jerks that Yiddish could not be shared, even with neighbor families, didn't become an absurd or terrible scene for me.

My grandfather's complaint—manifested in a dance that was at a certain point laughable, performed on one of the paths of that empty zoo—seemed like more of a joke than a protest.

He didn't show the tragic nature he truly carried within him.

It seems to me that this is the purpose of dance in general.

To conceal a series of unresolved ancestral questions that appear from generation to generation in situations that seem banal.

The prohibition against making his mother tongue public seemed to be the fundamental issue at the heart of the pantomime that my grandfather would always perform.

In that moment of apparent ecstasy, my grandfather even began to mispronounce his Spanish, which he usually could express himself with in a natural—what we would even call perfect—way.

I remember that he even mixed up the gender of his Spanish, uttering "*la* Yiddish," "*los* casitas," or "*los* welt completa," trying to say "the whole world."

Between songs, he said that on a certain occasion he disobeyed the order not to speak Yiddish beyond the confines of his family, making him the subject of ridicule by some of the children in his village.

I remember that he fled, and he walked, disconcerted, for some miles.

Finally he threw himself down in the middle of a wheat field and begged God to grant him death.

From then on (and it seems that he fulfilled this denial up until the moment when I saw him dancing at the zoo) he never uttered another word in his native tongue.

Until this moment, in which I find myself repeating the names of God almost without pause, it never occurred to me that something similar might have happened to Macaque.

That is, that she never used Yiddish except to recall the prohibition that weighed against that language.

I then saw Macaque living in an RV camper, which is where my grandfather said she had set herself up after the assassination of her martial arts fighter.

According to my grandfather, the camper was painted light blue, and time had eaten away at the tires.

It lay hidden in the foliage surrounding a park that, curiously, my grandfather told me was close to the zoo where we would visit the camels.

I'm not sure whether or not I asked him on any occasion if we could walk over there to meet that person that I had heard named so often face to face.

Macaque.

I would have liked to see not only Macaque, but also the blue camper she lived in.

I'm not sure if I ever asked my grandfather anything of that nature.

But I know that it would have been useful to do so, because my grandfather had knowledge that since the martial arts fighter's death, Macaque had become submersed in a deep state of melancholy.

If I had gone to visit Macaque, I would have also met another of the people who lived with her in the camper: Master Porcupine.

At this point things really start to get confusing.

Not even in my prayer cell, repeating the names entrusted to me by my order's sheikha, can I find any logical explanation for these occurrences.

Besides Macaque, my grandfather mentioned a few other characters.

The first that I remember is Master Porcupine.

My grandfather told me that Macaque had offered—in spite of the state of grief she found herself inundated in—to help Master Porcupine develop a theory that he called "Mariotic."

It had first occurred to him while giving math classes to students at a public school.

What is the Mariotic Theory?

It's precisely what I've come to ask myself now that I am in a state of prayer.

I remember that my grandfather partially explained it to me.

He explained that this theory was named after a writer.

Mario Bellatin.

Master Porcupine didn't try so much to understand the texts that this author had produced, but rather the mechanisms that he used to create them.

It was a situation for which the words written by that author would give rise to facts that indeed lay beyond the logic of things, but not beyond their nature.

Macaque had hung, on the inner wall of her camper, an old movie poster advertisement for a Bruce Lee film.

I find it incredibly curious that my grandfather would have referred—the version of the story that I offer here is completely faithful to that which my grandfather told me—to Bruce Lee during his never-ending descriptions of Macaque.

I find it impossible, because the image of my grandfather, standing before the camels at the zoo, is chronologically situated in the early years of the sixties, and everybody knows that the martial arts film genre didn't become popular until years later.

Nevertheless, the voice of my grandfather insisting that there was a Bruce Lee poster hanging on the wall of Macaque's camper only gets clearer with time.

The mention of a film of that nature makes me recall the success this movie had, primarily in those regions of the world where Yiddish was spoken fluently.

This fact is one that I am certain my grandfather told me.

There's no other way I could have obtained a fact of that nature: that the martial arts film genre had great success in those regions of the world where Yiddish was spoken fluently.

What places could that entail?

Where in the world could Yiddish still have been spoken as a native tongue?

I now know that the existence of such places is false.

In this cell where I find myself repeating the ninety-nine sacred names of God in a seemingly endless way, I know there are no regions in the world where that language is spoken fluently.

Therefore I also know that it is impossible that those alleged speakers of Yiddish could have been incommensurately enthused by martial arts films.

The affinity felt in the projection halls between those who used the prohibited language of my ancestors and the films that were in Chinese was impressive.

Some attendees even adopted certain Asian inflections that sounded like they came from their native language.

I think that having attended one of these functions would have given my grandfather great enjoyment.

Although I am sure that, given his manner of being, he wouldn't have given in to the catharsis into which many of his linguistic brothers fell.

As I've said, the sea was nearby.

It was even possible at certain times to clearly hear the breaking of the waves from the zoo.

On one of the occasions when we were together, my grandfather told me about the night that one of the seals had escaped from its pool and tried to make it back to the sea.

Bruce Lee's face presiding over the main wall of the camper stood out to Master Porcupine.

He asked a few questions.

Macaque clarified that the poster was an homage to her deceased lover.

That actor had been the fighter-turned-shoemaker's favorite.

Macaque thought that her lover had even had something to do with the film advertised on that poster hanging from the wall.

That fighter that she found in a roadside restaurant never confirmed whether or not he had been a personal friend of Bruce Lee.

Only sometimes he let signs of it slip.

On more than one occasion he shared details of the actor's life.

Of the relationships that Bruce Lee had with the mafia and how he had been sentenced to death, not just him but also his descendants for three generations.

The fighter-turned-shoemaker had lived for some years in the United States.

He had a habit of telling Macaque that he had come to control, of his own free will, a few million dollars.

It all ended when, from one moment to the next, he had to flee the country carrying only what he was wearing.

At the end of his stories the fighter always said the same thing: that Bruce Lee's perdition had come about because he was too committed to the material objects surrounding him.

Macaque purchased the poster—the one she had hanging from the main wall of her camper house—the very morning that they told her that the police had assassinated her lover.

She found it on her way back from the morgue she was required to visit.

As she walked down the street she suddenly saw, there on the sidewalk, Bruce Lee's face.

A street vendor had laid out a series of movie posters from every era of film on the floor.

What Master Porcupine was doing in the camper is a question I never dared to ask my grandfather.

I also know that he never would have answered me.

Mainly because my grandfather was a man of few words.

Jacob the Mutant (the book that precedes this text) was written by Joseph Roth in moments of inebriation.

It begins by confirming that it is a work that was never published during its author's lifetime.

For a variety of reasons, it was kept hidden until the time when certain retired employees of two German publishing houses admitted to having saved fragments of the text in their archives.

The Border.

Mario Bellatin gives these fragments the name *Jacob the Mutant*, and he selects those fragments in which Joseph Roth narrates the years of the tavern known as The Border, as well those spent in an American village.

Mario Bellatin himself has affirmed on more than one occasion that the material left by Joseph Roth is quite extensive and chaotic.

For example, in the book *Jacob the Mutant*, the Tiny Nocturnal Zoo is never mentioned.

The Tiny Nocturnal Zoo is a place similar to the one that my grandfather and I traversed on certain days of the week.

In my grandfather's zoo, in addition to the camels, there was a pool where some seals were being raised.

In the birdhouse for birds of prey something terrible would happen.

Because it was an establishment of meager means, some of the employees would be given orders to place cages in nearby trees, so as to trap small wild birds that would then be placed live in the same enclosures as the birds of prey, as food for them.

The Tiny Nocturnal Zoo was located next door to Rabbi Jacob's house.

On more than one occasion, Mario Bellatin affirmed that he found it fascinating to imagine a scene, in the early hours of the day, of a humble rabbi welcoming a set of children from a Central European village as his wife returned home after having run the tavern that they had set up in what had previously been, for several generations, the barn on the property where they lived.

The children were received in the main area of the small house. Around a large wooden table that Jacob and his wife used to eat.

It wasn't common in those days (nor do I think it is today) for rabbis to behave in such a way.

Not only was it unusual to receive children in their house instead of a classroom built outside of the home, but it was also strange that his wife would dedicate her time to managing an establishment of that nature.

That she would do it at improper hours, as well.

That the wife of a rabbi had to face a series of drunken men wasn't common within the tradition.

This is why the woman in reality managed a collection of trained wild animals—a nocturnal zoo, of sorts—which was the way the couple had found to carry out such an activity within the norms of their religion.

In that corner of the Austro-Hungarian Empire lay the rabbi's small house and the tavern—a nocturnal zoo— out back.

Even though it didn't have an established name, the establishment was known as The Border to the people who frequented it.

They were not easy times and, a few kilometers away— perhaps two or three—lay the Empire's outer limits.

It was a confusing region. In addition to the economic difficulties that had become a part of day-to-day life (which were the reason the barn had to stop being used for its original purpose and become a small zoo whose visitors could drink huge amounts of alcohol surrounded by caged wild animals), in neighboring Russia the pogroms that had devastated the region for several centuries had intensified, or—better put—come back.

The changes in the political situation in Russia appeared to have revived the systematic practice of the elimination of entire Jewish communities.

The news of villages laid waste by revolutionary forces had even reached the place where the Tiny Nocturnal Zoo was located.

The community members would get together in the rabbi's house to hear the stories brought by some of the survivors of that holocaust.

Around Jacob's table the sad tales were told, almost inevitably ending in a synagogue ablaze and the faithful trapped within.

Jacob always advised his visitors to continue their flight.

To take refuge as quickly as possible far from those lands.

Jacob knew that at a given moment not so far into the future the same occurrences would also come to the village they lived in, reason for which he took advantage of these reunions to remind his community members that they ought to perpetually be prepared for a diaspora.

Not only did the dispersion that his community members would suffer and the future of the children he was educating worry Jacob, but also the future of the Tiny Nocturnal Zoo that had cost him many years and much effort to build.

The Tiny Nocturnal Zoo was built little by little.

As is known, Jacob and his family lived in a region of continuous transit.

It was not uncommon that hunters from the north would cross the town, carrying with them the young of the wild animals they had killed for their furs.

Small wolf cubs, bears of various sizes, and small lion or tiger cubs were among the animals brought by those foreigners on their way through the region.

Gradually the barn became the place where Jacob himself built a series of cages to raise the animals he went about acquiring or trading for food items.

He liked to brag about a panther that as a cub had cost him the equivalent of twenty kilograms of recently harvested oats.

It was curious how, despite the fact that Jacob's words seemed as if they were filled with the logic of the obvious, many of his community members couldn't believe that at any point in time they would no longer belong to the land that had been theirs for several generations.

Jacob tried to be subtle while expressing his statements.

He understood that many of them, himself included, didn't have a thorough understanding of the world.

That is why he was extremely cautious when, upon finishing a cage, he would tell his followers: go forth and walk and try not to think.

Nonetheless, he urged those who came fleeing to continue their routes and not to stop until they reached some point on the other side of the ocean.

In the meantime, he managed to arrange—under the pretext of his visits to the Tiny Nocturnal Zoo—for his wife to carry forward the administration of the tavern while Jacob took on the responsibility of teaching the community children by day and caring for the animals, keeping them in the best conditions possible.

It was difficult for some to know what motive Jacob really had for keeping a tavern in operation.

Some could have thought that it had to do with a means of making money, but few understood that the real reason behind such an establishment was helping the numerous people fleeing the Russian pogroms so that they might escape to other lands.

Jacob not only dedicated his time to carrying out the responsibilities of a rabbi, maintaining a small zoo, and running a tavern, but also seemed to have a mission to save the lives of those in danger.

The first sign that times were also to change in the community where they lived came when he warned that the authorities put into place by the new regime (which had all been established while the large part of the inhabitants had no awareness of when exactly this had happened) began to act slightly differently than was normal.

Given that the town was situated in a somewhat far away location, it was difficult for recent news to reach them quickly.

This is why, suddenly, the inhabitants noticed that the uniforms of the soldiers who started to wander down their streets were different from those that had appeared in the past.

And not only that, but they also had to tolerate a series of harsh inspections that initially left them taken aback.

Then, calmly, the inhabitants went about growing to a certain extent accustomed to these initial changes.

Then a series of at times unexpected intrusions suddenly began to occur.

For example, the new civil servants developed a habit, just like that, of interrupting the classes Jacob gave to the village children, asking questions that appeared to be out of place.

Curiously, they never made an allusion to the tavern or the classes that he gave; their interest seemed to lie solely in the Tiny Nocturnal Zoo that he kept as a sort of attraction.

The agents of the new order kept placing increasing obstacles and demands on its operation.

They primarily cited reasons of a sanitary nature.

One morning the inspectors appeared after classes, and as Jacob's wife slept, they closed the establishment, giving its owner a pressing deadline to remove the animals.

Without the Tiny Nocturnal Zoo, it would be impossible for Jacob to continue with the routine that saw his wife spending her nights awake before a group of drunken men.

He wasn't just not going to be able to manage the tavern but not able either to provide shelter and help to those fleeing the pogroms carried out in the neighboring country.

Jacob then found himself facing a dilemma:

What to do with the wild animals?

He knew that in the Sacred Texts no great reference was made to them.

Save for Noah and his redeeming ark, he didn't know of the existence of a possible guide for divine precepts to follow, which could orient him on the matter.

As an initial measure, Jacob closed the whole tavern.

Not just the Tiny Nocturnal Zoo, as the authorities had ordered him to.

He retreated into his Torah studies, waiting for the moment when the agents of the new order would carry forth the final sentence: that is, what he had slowly been suspecting would occur to the members of his community at a relatively soon point in time.

Jacob continued to teach his pupils, to whom he had the habit of repeating, among other things, that any person who engaged with the Torah was capable of accepting the idea that he had the strength necessary to sustain the world on his own.

Of carrying upon himself each and every one of the objects of Creation, including, of course, animals.

Upon seeing the children's anxious faces, Jacob would tell them to keep up with their daily tasks because all work would be noted and tallied, as corresponded, as is appropriate and fit to occur.

Jacob's wife had accepted her job as manager of the tavern after a long night of theological debate with her husband as to whether or not such a position was acceptable.

It seems to me that on that occasion Jacob employed for the first time that idea that every tally would be tabulated as corresponds, as is appropriate and fit.

Jacob's wife would often remove her wig in the presence of her husband and cry when Jacob tried to convince her that an obligation of that nature was not at odds with the laws.

His wife felt that it was.

Jacob's wife wasn't capable of explaining it with words, but she was certain that spending entire nights dealing with men who were becoming drunk while watching a group of caged animals could not be seen as good by divine eyes.

For Jacob's wife there could be nothing divine in setting up the Tiny Nocturnal Zoo, whose real purpose was to hide the fact that a rabbi's wife was managing a tavern, all the while this tavern acted as a front for an operation to save the many lives of those who found themselves in danger.

As his wife cried, Jacob repeated to her that, within the community, it was not possible that any member of the human species existed without also possessing a corresponding entity.

With that he hoped to express to her that the Torah had already accounted for the fact that she was to administer the tavern.

What's more, he was trying to tell her that her mirror had already engaged in that activity since the beginning of time.

She (Jacob would say to her as he caressed her real hair), as a human being, was divided into parts, like stages, that at the same time were a reflection of other times in history.

The members of any community of believers were organized into parts of a single body.

In other words, Jacob seemed to want to tell his wife that she was not only his wife, but that she also represented a portion of a much more extensive body.

And not just that, Jacob informed her that this means of structure didn't correspond only to mankind but was also found throughout the entire world, including animals.

All creatures, Jacob would repeat to his disconcerted wife before she would accept her post running the tavern, are members upon members, some positioned over others, organized into one sole body.

And these beings, which at the same time form stages, are like the Torah, because the Torah is made up entirely of members and joints, *pirkin*, also known as sections or segments, that are always found some positioned above others, organized all of them and continuously functioning as one sole structure.

Despite finding myself before the story of Jacob and his wife, the manager of a tavern, despite seeing the house and the tavern—with its Tiny Nocturnal Zoo—rise up scant few kilometers from the border, it never stopped seeming weird to me (a curious reader of the Joseph Roth texts rescued from the archives of some German publishing houses) that a situation of this nature could arise. This situation was precisely one in which a rabbi, at whose hands the members of his community found themselves, insisted on making his wife become the manager of a tavern and, additionally, take on the responsibility of displaying a group of caged wild animals.

Both Jacob and his wife endured that process for quite some time.

As you could guess, Jacob's wife was not quickly convinced.

On more than one occasion Jacob appealed to the teachings of David, particularly the moment when David opened his eyes and said: *How innumerous, Lord, are your works!*

All of your works you created them with Great Wisdom...the Earth is full of your creatures (Psalms 104:24).

In the Torah, the celestial secrets are sealed and intangible—*de'la yakhlin lehitdabaka*, "they cannot be grasped"—Jacob kept telling his wife until one night, exhausted, she acquiesced, saying: *It is true, I have understood it, it is God's will that I be the manager of a tavern of lost men.*

The wife gave her acceptance immediately after Jacob informed her that in the Torah the celestial matters, both revealed and unrevealed, are one and the same.

The world is always the same.

The world of today and the world to come.

And in the Torah every possible word from every time is present.

Nevertheless, it cannot come to be that someone should be able to see them, control them or even know them, in the same way that the sheikha who manages the order to which I pertain hinted to me at the existence of each one of the ninety-nine names of God.

Nobody can see the names of God—both Jacob the Mutant and the sheikha of my order said.

This is perhaps the reason for which it is written: *Who can speak of the great works of the Lord? Who can sing His praises?* (Psalms 106:2).

What happened next was terrible.

Very soon the agents of the new order carried out what they had warned of and entered the barn violently, shooting each of the caged animals dead.

In that era of social disorder, many Russian brethren came through the village and managed to cross all of Europe until many of them reached the ports of the Mediterranean or the North Sea in aims of fleeing as far as possible.

Following the first incursion of the agents of the new order, Jacob sought out the services of a good taxidermist.

Jacob checked with the members of his community and learned that a distant cousin of his who lived in a relatively distant village specialized in that activity.

Jacob left on his search.

After a few days of investigating, he found him and, luckily, managed to convince him to stuff the beasts he had managed to maintain with such care in the Tiny Nocturnal Zoo.

But upon returning to his village, Jacob returned to the news that his wife had left him.

His wife had fled with someone—the young Anselm, who had helped her manage the tavern—a man who seemed to have very clear plans to reach the American continent as quickly as possible.

It would seem as though Jacob's words that the Torah looked with good eyes upon the wife of a rabbi managing a tavern had been so convincing that when that establishment closed to the public she realized that her life had no meaning at Jacob's side.

Upon hearing the news—all while the distant cousin made preparations to stuff the animals from the Tiny Nocturnal Zoo—Jacob tried to console himself faced with his loss by reciting out loud a passage from one of his Sacred Books:

When a human being climbs into bed it is first appropriate for him to somehow crown the Kingdom of Heaven and then recite a verse of loving kindness.

The companions who aided in the creation of the Zohar elucidated this: that when a human being sleeps in his bed, his soul abandons the body and wanders above.

The aforementioned companions never clarified what the blessed "above" meant.

Nevertheless, they pointed out that each and every soul did so—this wandering—according to its own manner.

After repeating these paragraphs a number of times, what Jacob did during this time was endlessly sleep.

That is the other fundamental passage that isn't found in the book *Jacob the Mutant*.

The one about Jacob's deep sleep.

Jacob perhaps held out hope that the moment would come when his soul would wander above and find a certain reason for his wife's conduct.

What is written? *In a dream, in a vision of the night* (Job 33:15).

Perhaps Jacob dedicated himself during those days to putting into practice this idea that when human beings lie down in their beds, they fall asleep and their souls leave them, as is written, *as they slumber in their beds*, then He, God, opens men's ears.

And thus, the Holy Blessed One tells the soul, through the grade or stage on which the poor soul stands, both the future of the Universe and matters of less transcendence.

According to his innermost thoughts—those disturbing or exhilarating thoughts, those that truly ought to be remembered, his mind must transform them into a transitory or momentary thought.

It is through these means that the human being is capable of traveling down the Universe's path of admonition.

Jacob knew that an angel had the information, who would at the same time transfer it to the soul and from the soul to the human being.

And this dream came from above, from the moment when the souls left their bodies and each one rose according to its manner.

As the cousin carried out his task in the most meticulous way possible, Jacob remained asleep.

And he didn't bring forward the sleep of the righteous, as one could expect.

He wasn't in that state of rest that both humans and animals tend to fall into in order to continue their customary habits.

I think of Jacob's sleep as somewhat similar to the state of remaining enclosed for two days in a prayer cell by the sheikha's order with the goal of repeating the ninety-nine names of God until exhaustion.

A state in which one is in a place of curious wakefulness.

A place where it is possible to find myself once again with my grandfather standing in front of a group of camels that display their dirt-covered backs, and to simultaneously discern the border town where Joseph Roth decided to place a tavern known as The Border.

A space where I can hear the absurd tales my grandfather would make up about Macaque and Master Porcupine.

It seems to me that only in a situation such as this one—finding myself enclosed in a prayer cell—could it be possible for me to imagine a poster like that of the film *Enter the Dragon*, with Bruce Lee as its protagonist.

I am certain that it was not the intent of my order's sheikha—when she suggested that I remain in a prayer cell to repeat the ninety-nine names of God in an interminable manner—for me to remember such a concrete phase of my childhood.

For me to hear yet again, in those circumstances, of the existence of a strange teacher who studied nothing less than a science that he had christened the Mariotic Theory.

In one of Joseph Roth's texts, long forgotten in those archives, it is written that Jacob tried more than once to explain to the children in his charge that the Merciful One—in this case, God—would be capable of forgiving them only if at some point in their lives they were in condition to explain Him.

That is to say, to give testimony to the existence of God Himself.

Nevertheless, giving testimony of the existence of God Himself is what I suspect my grandfather was doing with me during our visits to the camels.

Sometimes he told me that Macaque was not the character who lived in a camper in a park near the zoo where we took our walks, but a Slavic woman who some time later became the artist Norah Kimberley when she went to live in the United States.

I don't believe that my grandfather suffered from any type of mental imbalance that would make him constantly change the versions of his stories he would tell me.

Once he even used our entire walk around the zoo— our visit to the camels, to the seal pool, and the birds of prey preparing to hunt the small birds placed by zoo employees inside their cages—to tell me the details of the Mariotic Theory that Master Porcupine had tried to expound.

A study that, among other things, had cost Master Porcupine his job—the reason why he needed shelter in Macaque's camper.

As I realized, my grandfather never explained to me why Macaque threw her efforts behind protecting various people in the precarious home where she lived.

In some way, Macaque's intentions gave the impression of conforming to the ideas that Joseph Roth seemed to want to transmit in some of his work's passages.

Both my grandfather's Macaque and Joseph Roth's Jacob seemed to want to transmit the idea that knowledge of God couldn't be transferred to any but the modest, those who lacked the habit of getting angry, to the humble and to experts in awe.

That was what my grandfather's Macaque seemed to want to accomplish with Master Porcupine, just as Joseph Roth's Jacob wanted to accomplish with the children whose parents left them at the door to Jacob's house each morning.

As he carried out his work as a rabbi, just before they killed his animals and he would remain asleep for entire days, Jacob knew that the living conditions maintained for generations were very soon to change.

He knew that what he could teach the children under his instruction would be worth little.

He was convinced that many of them would end up dead at the least expected time.

The survivors would be dispersed and each one would be thrown to his fate.

They would go through life carrying wounds—both of the body and the soul.

Among other matters, Jacob knew that water was the element best fit for transferring knowledge.

Perhaps for this reason he carried out a series of curious ablutions before the bewildered gaze of the other community members.

The voice of the Lord is over the waters (Psalms 29:3).

In some way he gave the impression of trying to bring a representation of the Kabbalistic ritual bath into practice on a small scale.

In the Scriptures it says:

And before the Rabbi teaches his student, they shall bathe in water and they shall submerse themselves in forty se'ot.

A *se'ah* is a biblical measure the size of an egg.

Forty se'ot *is the minimum size for a* mikveh.

A *mikveh* is a ritual bath.

To carry out such an act they had to dress in white clothes and fast the entire day before the ritual.

The participants had to begin standing with the water reaching up to their ankles.

The rabbi would then open his mouth and with awe he would repeat his repetitive song:

Blessed are You, Lord, our God, King of the World. The Lord, God of Israel.

You are one and Your name is one, and You have ordered us to hide Your great name because Your name is wondrous.

Blessed are You and blessed is the name of Your glory forever, the glorified and wondrous name of the Lord, our God.

The voice of the Lord is over the waters.

Blessed are You, Revealer of Your secret to those who fear You.

God is the knower of secrets.

As these ideas went through my head (I remained confined in my prayer cell), Jacob remained sleeping, and his cousin focused on his labor of stuffing the bodies of the wild animals.

Many a person could inquire into the meaning of such a task.

For what reason could it be so important, for Jacob and for his cousin as well, to carry out this sort of homage to the Tiny Nocturnal Zoo, which for so many years simply served the purpose of disguising the existence of a tavern managed, in such a strange way, by the wife of a rabbi?

At that time, things began to get progressively worse in the community.

After having carried out relatively calm lives, many of the villagers began to be monitored and some of them even came to have signs hung from their necks that testified to their pertinence to the Jewish faith.

The children suddenly stopped going to the rabbi's house where they had sat around the large wooden table that also served its purpose as a dining room table.

If truth be told, the children suddenly stopped going to Jacob's house not only because of the steady escalation of things but also because the rabbi would spend his days sleeping.

The floods have lifted, O Lord, the floods have lifted up their voice; the floods have lifted up their roaring surge. Greater than the crash of many waters, greater than the mighty breakers of the sea, mighty is the Lord on high (Psalms 93:3–4).

The voice of the Lord is over the waters. The God of glory sounds, the Lord is over many waters (Psalms 29:3).

Jacob slept, and his cousin continued his labor.

Once the cousin finished giving certain positions to the animals' corpses (which, in some way, brought back memories of the times when the animals were still alive and were the attractions offered by the Tiny Nocturnal Zoo), that very cousin began to test out positions, with concrete actions, to give some grandeur to the scene of dead animals.

The cousin positioned the embalmed panther so it would be attacking the wild wolf.

The hyena, which a lost, wandering man had transported from Africa, bore a wide grin like that it was seen to have in its natural habitat.

Jacob, meanwhile, continued sleeping...

He couldn't seem to handle the abandonment he had just suffered in a state of wakefulness.

Jacob also couldn't seem to handle the fate of the Tiny Nocturnal Zoo or the atrocities occurring around him.

It is not known how, but during his sleep he was even able to learn that the dances particular to his community had begun to be prohibited.

Especially those dances of the Hasidic tradition that were usually performed twice a year on the outskirts of town.

The authorities resorted to taking measures based on a Roman text written in Latin, where more than two thousand years ago the same thing had been prohibited within the boundaries of Rome.

Cum progenitores nostri Christianæ Religionis cultores quæsīverint separationem Judæorum a Christianis, statuendo illis habitationem in Venetiis 15 dierum, & signum tellæ zallæ in medium pectoris, & Judæi variis ingeniis & fraudibus suis impetraverint non portare signum, se cum mulieribus Christianis immisceant, & Juvenes doceant sonare & cantare, tenendo publicas Scholas; Vadit pars, quod omnis Judæus non portans signum telæ zallæ, sine ulla gratia vel remissione condemnetur in pœna statuta. Et similiter aliquis Judæus non possit tenere Scholas alicujus ludiartis, vel doctrinæ, vel ballandi, vel cantandi, vel sonandi, vel docere aliter in civitate nostra, sub pœna Ducat. 50, & standi sex menses in carceribus. Liceat tamem illis mederi.

What was truly prohibited was the festive and rebellious nature of clapping and dancing.

According to tradition, dancing and clapping helped because a kind of mystical wind would blow through the heart that would help the participating souls reach the highest point that could be reached while on Earth.

A wind that was capable of penetrating the sixteen joints of the arm and the sixteen joints of the legs that all human beings have.

Recalling this, there in the prayer cell where I found myself, the words proclaimed by the sheikha of my order took shape, the ones where she affirmed that living bodies were morphologically prepared to receive the mystical experience.

That mysticism wasn't a question of faith, but rather the revelation itself of our living organism.

Something concrete and palpable.

In some way similar to how, when clapping or performing the traditional dances, the presence of the divine wind that lifted the heart's spirits became evident.

It seems to me then that the presence of the hundreds of dance academies that appear in the chapter "Beatitudes" of the book *Jacob the Mutant* isn't a casual occurrence.

In *Jacob the Mutant* there is an entire city full of dance schools.

A population that finds itself obliged—just as Rome was more than two thousand years ago—to impose a series of restrictions around that practice.

There Jacob can be found, living in that place after having fled the horror into which his homeland plunged.

Serving as a rabbi, carrying out his strange ablutions in a lake of pestilent waters found facing the lands given to him by his ship brother.

Anyone who has read the book knows that "ship brother" is the term that the immigrants used with each other, thus guaranteeing a pact of aid in survival at their shared destination.

These dances—neither in ancient Rome nor in the American settlement where Jacob and his family ended up living—could not be performed under the fate of free will.

According to what is written, one should turn to the presence of the righteous man—Hasidic or *ha-tzadik*, the name given to the leader of a Hasidic group—so he may guide them.

And there was Jacob Pliniak until, suddenly, as if being called upon by one of the Mystical Sephirot that only present themselves to certain beings once in a lifetime, as he carried out his usual ablutions in the waters of the region's lake, he came back to the surface, transformed into an old woman named Rose Plinianson, a Catholic woman who until just before her death put all of her efforts behind fighting the dance academies that threatened to annihilate the city where they lived.

A case of transmutation similar to the one that my grandfather tried to show me each time he brought me to visit the camels?

An occurrence of transformation like that which my grandfather carried out when from one day to the next he was no longer at my side?

Let not the foot of pride overtake me (Psalms 36:12).

While the feet are raised through dance, the ego lessens in intensity, seems to be what Jacob Pliniak repeated as he submersed himself in the waters before coming back out transformed into the young Miss Plinianson.

The more that we wash our feet, the ga'ava—*ego*—*is nullified in a very effective way.*

That American community couldn't have known—here from my prayer cell I am certain of this—that the dances performed according to certain premises also help nullify idol worship.

Idolatry, and not monotheism, in that city of the Far West, so far from the centers of theological debate?

Jacob understood through his readings of the Books that in those moments when the permanence of the idea of monotheism stood on shaky ground, Hasidic leaders brought their villagers, in any way possible, to spaces favorable to dance.

The leaders should not offer great explanations to make their people dance.

It was enough for them to congregate in the main city squares and voice the phrase:

Wash your feet (Genesis 18:4).

But under the conditions the village found itself in—here we are referring to that place where Jacob was asleep, where his tavern was located—it was impossible, due to the new order's incursion, to carry out any activity capable of bringing that spiritual wind to their hearts.

The only secret task was that which the cousin was carrying out in the solitude of what had once been the shed of Jacob's house.

Upon hearing of the proclamations outlawing dancing, which were being hung up on the main walls of the village, the cousin couldn't think of any idea better than making a tiger dance with a seal (which some poor man had brought Jacob from the Russian seas).

The cousin's stuffed animals began to dance in a sort of ecstatic parody of movement.

As the prohibitions for the community members increased, the animals of the Tiny Nocturnal Zoo performed the most bizarre dance steps one could imagine.

Rounds of penguins, *dhikrs*—ancestral dances—made up of glass-eyed orangutans.

This far along into the new reality that the village was living, the inhabitants—one by one, even the most timid—understood that they were being called upon so that a luminous wind would reach their hearts, one which can only be brought about by lifted feet.

But the lifting of feet that the inhabitants of the village were being called to was not that which was usually obtained through dance—that is to say, that which tradition had prescribed—but rather the new members of the order arrived with the gospel that that state would only be reached through labor—the only action capable of liberating men.

Only labor will set you free, seemed to be the contemporary declaration.

For that purpose, the authorities invited the villagers to prepare their bags with the most basic items in advance.

They were then driven to the train that would take them to the promised paradises.

Many believed that they were being called upon not only to carry out a task of physical purification, but also that they were being summoned to carry out a true prayer.

They furthermore believed—let's not forget that we are discussing a community composed of simple beings, many of whom spent their nights drunk in that tavern managed by the rabbi's wife—that they were called upon to practice a prayer that reached such lofty heights that, at that point, it was not possible to demand any further explanation.

In other words—standing sorted into the lines that were congregating at the train station—they thought that they were invited to carry out an action that, in those moments, it was impossible to comprehend.

They had the understanding as well that, in order to do what was being requested of them, they ought to carry out an activity similar to some form of corporeal liquidation—*lehitpashtut hagashmiut*—which in other terms means "to shed one's body."

Finally the members of that small community were taken into account by somebody other than themselves.

Throughout the centuries they had been a forgotten part of the Empire and now, finally, the inhabitants held an importance for someone other than God.

They no longer merely formed part of a Divine—and consequently, intangible, as Jacob had informed them on more than one occasion—Plan, but they now belonged also to a project invented by men, ones who had taken up the work of noticing their existence.

It was precisely in this moment that what we could identify as a sort of social ecstasy appeared, and under the sunlight of that spring morning the colorful parade of neighbors could be seen, each person carrying his or her own suitcase.

While this all was occurring, Jacob continued to sleep, and his cousin continued on with his task of making the dead animals dance.

What happened next is history.

When Jacob awoke, the village was almost empty.

Not a soul could be spotted in the streets.

The businesses and the synagogue—shut down.

Where are our Catholic brothers? Jacob dared ask.

It seems as though they, too, had left.

That they were not in the village despite remaining present.

According to what Jacob later found out (this passage doesn't appear in the work *Jacob the Mutant*) many of the villagers continued on there in the village, carrying out their normal daily labors and yet Jacob was incapable of seeing them.

Could this phenomenon of the transparency of outside bodies be related to a variation of the many Sephirot that we men tend to fall into when our souls are thus attuned?

In reality, the only ones who had left the village were those individuals who, up until a few weeks prior, had been required to wear a sign around their necks.

But for Jacob that place was nothing more than a ghost town.

Jacob observed this from his bedroom window.

Next to his window stood the empty bed, left behind just a month earlier by his wife.

When Jacob left home and approached the shed, he could see his cousin in the midst of the dance that, at that point, he had spent days arranging.

Despite being a static dance by nature, the cousin took charge of frequently varying it.

When he felt that the ostrich had been dancing with the rabbit for too long, he would—quite suddenly—switch their partners.

At a certain point, Jacob touched the cousin on his back and told him that it was time to set out for the diaspora.

To help him place the stuffed animals into the wagon where he had once transported the Russian fugitives.

He urged him to then follow, without wasting any time, the paths he knew so well by memory from having trafficked so many people while the tavern was running.

After a few unexpected events they arrived, all the while pulling the wagon, to one of the ports ships departed from.

There the cousins were faced with a dilemma: the two of them could not travel with the wagon on the same boat.

There wasn't enough space.

Either the two of them could travel together and leave the wagon at the port, or just one could go while the other waited for the next departure, which would set sail with more space.

Jacob boarded the first ship alone.

There, on that trip, he became ship brothers with the man who would later give him the lands where he was to take roots with his recovered wife—as is known, once in New York Jacob convinces his former wife to return to him—in front of a lake situated in a city overcrowded with dance academies.

His cousin boarded the second ship, which left ten days later, with the wagon with those animals that once made up the Tiny Nocturnal Zoo.

But something happened at sea.

Mid-voyage the notice came that Jacob's ship would be the last to be granted entry into the United States without visas for its passengers.

As a result, the cousin's ship docked in Veracruz.

This is the reason why the stuffed animals remain until this day in the basement of a house on Calle Ideal in Mexico City, a place where the taxidermist cousin eventually ended up settling down.

Affairs with Respect to *Jacob the Mutant* that It Would Be Good Not to Forget or Leave to Chance

It seems important to me that any interested party, having arrived at this point of the book *Jacob the Mutant* as of the text that attempts to respond to the relevance of having written it, keep in mind a set of elements that I, as author, hold under consideration.

When my grandfather would refer to Master Porcupine at the zoo, he would always give me some new explanation or other about the Mariotic Theory being developed by that teacher.

Master Porcupine always wore a black felt hat.

In my memories my grandfather would refer to that hat with precision.

He would describe its particularities with such detail.

I found it curious that he would do this—with such precision, no less—given that my grandfather always walked around bareheaded.

This is why the blond fuzz that grew from his ears was so visible.

On more than one occasion he said that from the time he arrived in the city where we were living, he had come to lose every hat that he had tried to start wearing.

It seemed as though his inability to wear a hat was some sort of a vengeance.

I think he even expressed as much to me on one occasion.

That thought—my grandfather's embarrassment for not wearing a hat, as was the custom—came to me fleetingly in one instant of the prayer I was immersed in.

At that moment I thought of something that seemed absurd: that my grandfather had slowly gone about losing his hats as a sort of vengeance for not having been able to ever pronounce a word in his mother tongue.

In that curious instant that took over me in my prayer cell I would have liked to have learned not just the reasons why my grandfather would constantly lose his hats, but also with what exact words my grandfather made his plea to God—lying in an open field sown with wheat—for Him to assist him in dying.

Perhaps these words do not exist, but if they possessed some kind of materialization, it would certainly be found represented in the hats that my grandfather endlessly lost.

My grandfather told me that Master Porcupine was unexpectedly fired from the elementary school where he worked.

He was accused of not following the program of studies, as well as using his students as guinea pigs to test what the school administrators felt was a strange theory, with the goal of systematizing it.

At the end of each month, Master Porcupine answered the questions on his students' exams himself.

He would also do their homework.

He would then turn in the papers to the administration as a progress report for his class.

The Mariotic Theory, according to Master Porcupine:

Something that occurs each time a minimal, isolated incident breaks with an established order, followed by the emer-

gence of a chain of uncontrollable chaos and increasingly absurd acts.

As my grandfather told me many times in front of the camels, it seems that *Enter the Dragon* was Bruce Lee's most successful film.

Macaque had never seen it.

No matter how many times her lover, the martial arts fighter, insisted she do so.

The movie was so successful that it continued showing for months at one movie theater downtown.

Macaque always answered the fighter, saying that she didn't enjoy movies with violence.

She had already had enough of that in the marriage that she had had to flee from behind her husband's back.

In those days Macaque and the martial arts fighter lived in the room they rented in that boarding house.

It was there that the news came of the death of her lover.

Macaque immediately walked out to the street.

The shoemaker's workshop was a few blocks away.

The corpse had already been taken to the city morgue.

Some police officers were still around.

Some were carrying handkerchiefs tied over their noses.

It was the first time that Macaque visited the workshop.

The shoemaker had forbidden it.

Macaque saw that it had two roofed sections and a small patio.

The first part was for displaying the shoes.

They were outdated models, simple, that nevertheless sought to respect a certain classic style.

They were displayed on wooden shelves.

At that time there were six pairs lined up.

In the same room were the working tools: a harness maker's tools, enormous scissors, thread, and sewing materials.

On the floor, stacked on top of each other, there was a pile of soles of various sizes.

The back room was set up as a bedroom for those nights when the fighter wasn't let in to the boarding house.

In one corner there was a bed covered with tulle netting that hung from the ceiling.

Opposite that a thread that hung from one side of the wall to the other.

Approximately one-and-a-half meters away from that thread some pieces of raw meat were hanging.

Below each piece there were some metal boxes, each with a hatch on top and a thin metal tube that went from the piece of meat to the cage's opening.

At the slightest movement the meat fell, bringing with it the entire animal and instantly closing the opening to the cage.

Rats, whose skin we know was used to make the shoes, would crawl in at night to eat those bits of meat, and they would fall into the boxes without any chance of escape.

Each night the fighter captured four or five animals.

The next morning he would butcher them on the back patio.

He would bring them out alive, and with a wooden stick he gave them a light blow to the snout that would kill them instantly.

He would then open their stomachs with a special knife, and with his pinky finger—whose nail he kept quite long for this sole purpose—he would rip out their entrails.

In that particular state of perception, doubtlessly motivated by the thousands of times I had already repeated the names of God, it occurs to me that my grandfather would have never accepted a pair of shoes made by a martial arts fighter.

My grandfather was an incredibly scrupulous dresser.

He was one of those people who only have one change of clothing, but of the highest quality.

Enter the Dragon had not only been the most commercially successful film, it was also that fighter-turned-shoemaker's favorite.

Macaque even believed that her lover had been involved in the creation of the film.

On more than one occasion that fighter had made references to personal details of the actor's life.

He spoke about the contacts he maintained with the Chinese mafia, one of the bloodiest mafias known.

Aside from the gated rattraps, in one corner of the patio there was a series of regular traps.

Some skins in the process of being treated were kept on a table.

Macaque was summoned to the morgue to identify the body.

One of the officers accompanied her.

On the way back to the boarding house she suddenly saw her dead lover's face in the middle of the sidewalk.

That face was there, on top of a pile of martial arts movie posters.

When she approached the vendor to ask about it, they told her it was the actor Bruce Lee.

Macaque found the portrait identical to her lover.

She had never seen Bruce Lee's face before.

She purchased the poster, and it is that poster that now hangs in the camper where she lives.

On a certain occasion I remember having asked my grandfather if the zoo had a closing time.

My grandfather answered that of course it did, for it was strange to come across someone who could focus on nature while working in the dark.

I remember that he told me this while throwing a candy into the seal pool.

One should never visit a zoo at night, was what he told me at first.

Although after a few minutes he told me that he remembered during his childhood it was known that in a nearby village there was a saloon that had a zoo that only showed its animals at night.

Nonetheless, he indicated that the inhabitants of the village where he lived found this strange.

My grandfather never thought of going to visit the camels by night.

They were old animals.

Their fur was matted.

They barely even moved.

Their nights must have been even sadder.

A particular kind of sadness.

Perhaps similar to that which I thought I saw appear on my grandfather's face when any allusion was made to his prohibited native tongue: Yiddish.

After having spent nearly thirty hours in my prayer cell at the advice of the sheikha of my Sufi order, I suddenly remembered that my grandfather told me how on a certain night that they spent awake past their normal bedtime, Macaque confessed to Master Porcupine that she had kept the proof necessary to show that Bruce Lee had not died a natural death.

That she was certain that her assassinated lover was Bruce Lee himself.

Nonetheless, for the American police, the case of the actor's death was closed.

My grandfather told me that Macaque began to tell Master Porcupine the true story of Bruce Lee in Yiddish: the language of his ancestors.

When I tried to tell him that that was not possible I felt that suddenly my grandfather began to disappear.

I don't know how to explain this process properly.

There, before the camels covered in dust, my grandfather, the one I'd always known, the one who took me on these walks, began to fade before my very eyes.

As though a higher force were erasing him from an imaginary piece of paper he had been drawn on.

Nevertheless, this type of disappearance of the image of my grandfather next to me does not mean that he ceased to be present.

No.

He was there without being there in reality, and without being an animal or plant or mineral substance either.

Maybe this is why the separation was not so traumatic for me.

My grandfather—in spite of the phenomenon that I began to perceive—was there, at my side, grasping my arm.

Many a person can ponder the relationship that might exist between this text I am now writing and the book *Jacob the Mutant* that precedes it.

The mystery could lie in the idea that stayed with me for many years, that my family thought that my grandfather could have transformed into some kind of animal, plant, or mineral.

But no, as I said, my grandfather seemed to find himself situated in a perpetual present, one in which a string of different languages—both living and dead—were able to converge on a single point: him.

And only in a present of this nature was the apparition of the Sacred Sephirot, as well as the idea that there is no God but God and nothing exists outside of Him.

Not even a seal fleeing toward the sea could provoke such an occurrence.

Some might even ask themselves how it was possible that Jacob wasn't needed for labor the way that the other inhabitants of his town were.

He wasn't called upon by the forces of the new order because he remained asleep for the duration of that season.

As though floating within the liquid that contains the columns that sustain the world.

In any case, questions about the perennial survival of Jacob will have to be asked of the English investigator who rescued the remains of the manuscripts from the German publishers.

I also don't believe we will ever know Master Porcupine's reasons for trying to develop his Mariotic Theory

Likewise, if the martial arts fighter was indeed Bruce Lee himself.

In the meantime, as these and other mysteries are slowly elucidated, the only thing left as something tangible is this book, *Jacob the Mutant*.

The aforementioned work and the group of camels that I used to visit with my grandfather before he disappeared from my life forever.

All the while I should not forget that, when I finish this state of prayer I find myself submersed in, the *tasbih*— that type of Muslim rosary—ought to be saved as if it were a relic.

Set next to a group of hardboiled eggs, like those prepared in the Catholic Church each afternoon.

A prayer rosary—*tasbih*—that, in some way, could bring the reader closer to the mystery that only the vision of a group of sheep grazing among rocks is capable of creating.

Let us have faith in it.

The Wait

The forms remain in suspense. The men's skin perpetually wet. A golem. A dozen boiled eggs. The Stroemfeld publishing house's employee, trying to blot out the traces of the text. No mutation is produced. All that appears is the image of some sheep grazing among rocks.

Explanatory Map, Number 2
by Zsu Szkurka

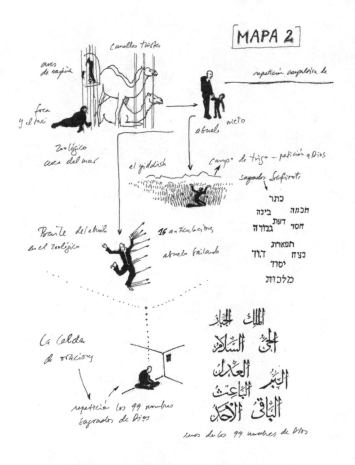

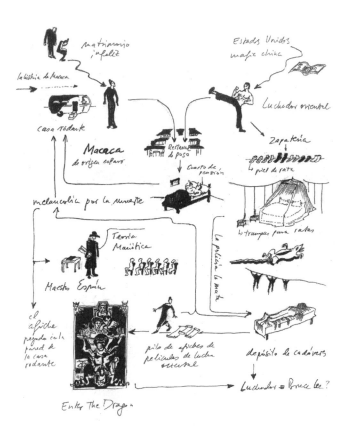

matrimonio infeliz

Estados Unidos
mafia china

la historia de Macaca

Luchador oriental

casa rodante

Zapatería

Macaca
de origen esclavo

Restaurant de paso

La piel de rata

Cuarto de pensión

melancolía por la muerte

las trampas para ratas

Teoría Maniática

La policía lo mata

Maestro Espía

el afiche pegado en la pared de la casa rodante

pila de afiches de películas de lucha oriental

depósito de cadáveres

Luchador = Bruce Lee?

Enter The Dragon

117

The Diary of Rose Eigen:
A Translator's Afterword

by Jacob Steinberg

Someone who maintains a routine life in his or her existence could perhaps have difficulties understanding
some of the occurrences in the text *Jacob the Mutant*.
Difficulties not only in understanding the characters,
but also the fates, the physical or geographical spaces,
and even the words that the reader must face. Each one
of these elements, among other aspects, seems to avoid
any aspect related to stability.

By writing these—now lost—texts whose rescued and
compiled fragments that have been rescued and compiled make up a portion of the book we now call *Jacob
the Mutant*, the writer Joseph Roth gives the impression
of having created a world inhabited by characters with-

out fixed identities, a universe that seeks to give way to new contexts, to realities that the reader unfamiliar with such forms—mentioned more than once in the book as aphoristic transformations—could deem absurd, or completely lacking sense.

But I know that there exist readers who understand—even some who have no alternative other than to understand—and know how such transformations work. They seem to understand them for the mere reason that they, themselves, have experienced similar mutations in the occurrences of their own lives.

Until recently I—now the book's translator into English—didn't have a precise idea of what it was that attracted me to such a text. I recall being overly intrigued by the somewhat strange occurrences that allegedly occurred in that border zone of the Austro-Hungarian Empire, events that gave way to the migration of a good number of Jewish immigrants to New York City, the place where I currently find myself writing this text.

In 1907, in New York City, a woman was born by the name of Rose Eigenmacht. Rose was the daughter of Charles and Yetta, immigrants from Eastern Europe (as were the greater part of the Jews who had settled in New York in that period). According to the gravesite of her parents—still today a tombstone bearing their names, both in

English and Hebrew, and their dates of birth and death continues to watch over the plot they share in a cemetery in the Borough of Queens—they were members of the Independent Skoller Lodge #220, a Jewish fraternal society for travelers who had come from the Galician city of Skole, territory of the Austro-Hungarian Empire.

I don't remember many other details I may have acquired regarding Rose's childhood. In fact, until just about seven or eight years ago, I didn't even know her name.

According to the data taken in the national censuses of the era, around the end of the Great War, Rose changed her last name to the shorter (and less German) Eigen.

In June of 1926, she married Benjamin Steinberg. One year later they had a son. Benjamin was also the child of Jewish immigrants, but unlike Rose, who had been born in these lands, Benjamin's parents brought him to this continent at three years of age.

Benjamin was seven years older than Rose. When they married, she was nineteen years old.

The family lived in a building on the Lower East Side. In those days the Lower East Side was the main area where one could find Jewish boarding houses.

It was around 1930 or 1931 that everything shifted. That year Rose had an affair with the superintendent of their building. Upon finding out about the affair, Benjamin divorced her, winning sole custody of their son.

Benjamin began to cut up the family photos. He made the bizarre decision to keep the photos that featured Rose, simply removing her face, perhaps so the eyes of that woman whom he hated so much couldn't be seen.

Very soon after, Benjamin replaced Rose with another woman, for the moment more faithful.

The only persistent reminder of Rose's existence for the new family was her monthly visits to the son she shared with Benjamin.

Despite the visits, the father taught his son to gradually come to despise his biological mother.

It may be difficult to believe—decidedly more difficult for those uninitiated in the art of the transmigration of souls—but I, Jacob Steinberg, the English translator of *Jacob the Mutant*, am the reincarnation of that woman, Rose Eigen.

Perhaps I should also make note here that I am her great-grandson.

To better understand the history between Rose and me, maybe I should divide it into mutations.

I believe that the first occurred when my great-grandfather cut up the family photos, leaving only Rose's faceless silhouette, and almost completely replaced the figure of Rose with that of his second wife, whom he married quite shortly after having been cheated on.

It is for that reason that my grandfather, Rose's son, acted as though Benjamin's second wife had been his mother.

It seems that the hostility ran so deep that his father taught him to never refer to his mother by name.

That is why for a good portion of my life I only had an intuition that such a woman formed a part of my family.

I had heard certain allusions, loose facts that clued me in to her existence in the family tree.

Many years had to go by before my grandfather, a nearly eighty-year-old man, felt the inexplicable need for me—his grandson—to at the very least know that woman's name.

The loose details that I previously knew about that woman, scant as they were, had always been an obsession for me.

When my grandfather revealed her full name to me, I immediately looked for her in the City Municipal Archives.

I researched her parents, the addresses where they lived, and information about the children her brothers and sisters may have had. Perhaps I was searching in those relatives for some memories that somehow belonged to me—memories that I had the purpose of recovering.

My paternal grandmother (who divorced Rose's son over fifty years ago) was the one who told me the story of Rose (whose name even my grandmother never knew) in more detail.

In her memory remained the fact that, shortly after having been married, she received a letter by mail containing a photograph and a letter.

It turned out to be a missive from her husband's mother, something that seemed exceedingly peculiar given that there was another woman that she believed was her mother-in-law.

The groom's mother, introduced as such, had been in the wedding, and it wasn't possible that her husband had two mothers.

Upon opening the envelope, my grandmother came across a missive and a recent photograph of one Rose Eigen.

Despite the fervor with which my grandmother narrated this incident to me, my grandfather completely denies it.

He does uphold that he stopped seeing his mother after turning eighteen years old—the point at which he and his father were no longer legally obligated to welcome that woman in their home.

My grandmother recalls that her father-in-law, Benjamin Steinberg, was present when she received the envelope, and upon learning of the contents of the envelope, he ripped the photo and the letter to shreds and then threw them into the lit fireplace.

Some might think that the years I spent trying to investigate the details of the life of my great-grandmother were sad ones.

Nevertheless, the chiaroscuro of that character and of how she was presented was, for me, essential. I immersed myself at that time in the mystical studies of my religion, in the body of spiritual knowledge known as the Kabbalah. Furthermore, I experienced a series of important relationships—two in particular—in which I was emotionally shattered by unfaithful men, men who left me to pursue their romantic flings.

At that point in my life, I questioned, among other things, the biophysical structures that define the limits of the body, the ability of two beings to trust in each other and become one. I even came to question something else: the supposed evil of that woman, my ancestor, Rose Eigen. I began to see her as a somewhat embittered and depressed figure, as a young woman who, in moments of extreme ecstasy (comparable to Hasidic dancing) exceeded her structural limits and, as a consequence, missed out on one of the possible lives that awaited her.

The issue around Rose is complicated.

The avid reader must certainly already recognize certain similarities between my great-grandmother's story and that of the book *Jacob the Mutant*.

Both the wife of Joseph Roth's Jacob and my great-grandmother Rose are women who cheat on their husbands, becoming involved with men who are significantly younger (in Rose Eigen's case, the superintendent of the building where she and her family lived; in the case of the rabbi's wife, the young Anselm who helped run the tavern).

I find another commonality between my life and *Jacob the Mutant*: the mystical influence of the Kabbalah, which played a central role both in Jacob Pliniak's training and during my years of formal academic research.

Furthermore, the transformation of one woman into another, both in the case of the actress Norah Kimberley and in the two wives who appear in Benjamin Steinberg's family photographs.

Both the author of the book and I, you could say, are people investigating the truth, searching for it within textual fragments contained in different archives.

I'd like to digress here and mention another event that transpired in my personal life. Something independent from my work as the translator of the book *Jacob the Mutant*.

Approximately one year has lapsed since I had my palm read by one who was an expert in those matters, the daughter of a well-known Kabbalistic rabbi. At the time, I did not know much about that woman's talents; I was merely certain that she possessed an unmatched talent.

Many details about my life were revealed to me during the course of our session. Details pertaining both to this present life and to others that I don't remember with precision.

I'd like to share one aspect in particular. The woman spent a great deal of time observing one particular small, curving line. A line that connected my middle finger with my ring finger on my right hand. According to chiromancy, this line indicated that I had a *tikkun*—a Hebrew word that implies a type of cosmic burden or correction—to be made in this lifetime with men who cheat on their spouses.

She told me that it wasn't that I was necessarily willing to have affairs, but that that line told her that I did have a tendency to forgive unfaithful men, to love them, even perhaps to the point of actively seeking them out in the wake of some infidelity.

Any believer knows that the lines of the palm are not a decree, but he also knows that the Creator makes no mistakes at the time when He determines how each and every one of us shall be formed.

It would take me another year or so to connect the dots and realize the evident implications of what the Kabbalistic palm reader sought to tell me.

That discovery happened as I was finishing my translation of a secondary text put together by Mario Bellatin to conclude a new Spanish edition of *Jacob the Mutant*.

There were so many readers fascinated by the events surrounding the compilation of those textual fragments of Joseph Roth's novel *The Border* that the compiler himself, Mario Bellatin, felt obligated to write another text about those elements of Roth's manuscript that did not make it (for some reason or another) into the first Spanish edition of the book.

As I went over the events that make up Jacob Pliniak's biography—as well as that of his stepdaughter, Rose, both of whom are one and the same in this work of fiction—I once again took up my search for details regarding Rose Eigen.

Slowly I came to the realization that I am the reincarnation of Rose Eigen.

Since a young age, I've felt an undeniable and inexplicable draw to my Jewish roots. Something made all the more curious by the fact that I so much more easily could have remained within the Lutheran tradition inherited from my maternal side.

I could have maintained a connection similar to that into which Rosalyn Plinianson entered with Reverend MacDougal following her transformation.

From a young age I also felt the pressing and somewhat illogical need to live in New York City, perhaps guided by a need to recover some element of my familial past.

In the theology of reincarnation, as conceived of by the Kabbalists, the soul undergoes a constant process of transformation.

The Kabbalists assert that souls go through similar circumstances time and time again until they eventually correct each one of their flaws.

Although oftentimes the circumstances that accompany a reincarnation only exist for the sake of impeding the correction—or, *tikkun*—necessary for the soul to complete its reincarnation cycle and finally gain access to the Garden of Eden.

I'm unaware of the date on which Rose Eigen died. I only know that like Jacob Pliniak—the Galician rabbi who had to cross many borders in order to transmute into his stepdaughter, Rose Plinianson—Rose Eigen's soul, too, had to wander. It had to be reborn into another life, one in which it would almost feel obligated to translate the contemporary writer Mario Bellatin. In this life, it appeared to be one of Rose Eigen's missions to spread the doctrine of the Mariotic Theory to the English-speaking world.

The Mariotic Theory: *Something that occurs each time a minimal, isolated incident breaks with an established order, followed by the emergence of a chain of uncontrollable chaos and increasingly absurd actions.*

But is it so absurd that a woman who was denied forgiveness would have to reincarnate as her own great-grandson?

That she would return to this world to face off against unfaithful men and a series of doubts about the religion of her ancestors?

In another of the epilogues that I wrote for this translation (a text that, now that I am looking for it, I cannot find in any complete document; only fragments of it appear in various journals and folders), I said that the only mechanism for making sense of *Jacob the Mutant* was to give in to its perpetual state of transformation. To remain always a reader in continuous mutation.

I recall, too (although these texts have become somewhat blurry in my memory), having written something about the temporal, geographic, and linguistic borders that we must cross all the time in order to continue on with our lives in the way that they've been assigned to us.

BIOGRAPHIES

Mexican writer **MARIO BELLATIN** has published dozens of novellas on major and minor publishing houses in Latin America, Europe, and the United States. Phoneme Media has published his novella *Shiki Nagaoka: A Nose for Fiction*, and will publish three more of his books through 2016, including *The Uruguayan Book of the Dead*, for which he won Cuba's 2015 José María Arguedas Prize. Bellatin's current projects include Los Cien Mil Libros de Bellatin, his own imprint dedicated to publishing 1,000 copies each of 100 of his books.

JACOB STEINBERG was born in Stony Brook, New York, in 1989. A poet, translator, and critic, his publications include *Magulladón* (2012) and *Ante ti se arrodilla mi silencio* (2013). As a translator, he has worked with Sam Pink, Luna Miguel, and Mario Bellatin, among others. Scrambler Books released his first English-language collection, *Before You Kneels My Silence*, as well as the first volume of his translations of contemporary Argentine poet Cecilia Pavón. He currently lives in New York.

ZSU SZKURKA is a Hungarian illustrator whose work explores the space between science and art. As a doctor that specializes in mental illness, her work explores the human form as observed in morgues, asylums, and sanitoriums, both in Hungary and Mexico, where she resides.